"What do you know about my affairs?" Lawson asked harshly.

"Why, nothing," she said at once. "I'm simply—assuming."

"Well, don't," he snarled. "That's where people get things wrong—by assuming. Why are women so infernally nosy?" he continued accusingly. "Why can't they leave well alone? If you know what's good for you, Caron, you won't mention my past again. It's over, it's done with, and I don't want reminding of it."

Born in the industrial heart of England, Margaret Mayo now lives with her husband in a pretty Staffordshire canalside village. A former secretary, she turned her hand to writing, setting her stories both at home and in exotic locations, combining her hobby of photography with her research.

Don't miss any of our special offers. Write to us at the following address for information on our newest releases.

Harlequin Reader Service
U.S.: 3010 Walden Ave., P.O. Box 1325, Buffalo, NY 14269
Canadian: P.O. Box 609, Fort Erie, Ont. L2A 5X3

INTRIGUE
Margaret Mayo

Harlequin Books

TORONTO • NEW YORK • LONDON
AMSTERDAM • PARIS • SYDNEY • HAMBURG
STOCKHOLM • ATHENS • TOKYO • MILAN
MADRID • WARSAW • BUDAPEST • AUCKLAND

ISBN 0-373-17216-8

INTRIGUE

Copyright © 1993 by Margaret Mayo.

CHAPTER ONE

CARON'S honey-blonde hair streamed out behind as she clung to the runaway horse. As the forest grew denser branches tore at her hair and clothes. She was forced to lie low on the mare's back and could feel the moist heat of the animal's sweat-lathered body, could almost smell the fear that pulsed through the scared creature with every pounding step, ears well back, stride long.

Her throbbing heart threatened to rob her of breath, her knees, pressed into the animal's sides in a supreme effort not to be thrown, ached with the constant pressure, her arms ached, everything ached. And nothing she could say or do stopped the mare's thundering hoofs.

The man came from nowhere. A giant of a man who took in the scene in one fleeting glance, throwing himself at the horse, hanging on to the halter, pitting his strength against that of the racing animal. Black hair he had, black and curly, that was all Caron noticed. He spoke to the animal as he was half dragged, half ran beside her, words that meant nothing to the girl on the horse's back and yet miraculously soothed the rampaging beast.

Within seconds of the man's appearance the mare slowed and stopped and Caron felt the tenseness go out of the animal, yet her own fingers refused to let go of the mare's mane, every bone in her body locked.

'You can get down now.'

The curt tones filtered into her haze of shock but although Caron looked at the stranger she was still unable to move.

He gave a snort of anger and with his hard-fingered hands spanning her waist he lifted her down, dumping her on the floor with as much ceremony as if she were a sackful of potatoes.

Caron's legs threatened to buckle beneath her; only by reaching out and supporting herself against the furious man did she manage to stop herself from falling into an ignominious heap at his feet.

There was no compassion in him. Within seconds he had pushed her savagely away and ruthless anger blazed out of eyes that were an intense shade of blue, followed swiftly by the cutting edge of his voice. 'You do realise your stupidity could have killed that horse?' Not a word about herself! 'If you're not capable of handling such an excitable animal you shouldn't be riding.'

Caron could not believe that this man was condemning her so absolutely. Did he not care that she might be shaken, that she had probably been more scared than the mare who was now contentedly cropping grass a few yards away? That she could have killed herself, never mind the horse? What sort of a man was he that he could think more of the animal than he did her?

'I am an accomplished rider,' she told him coldly. 'It wasn't my fault that she bolted.'

'But yours that you hadn't the experience to control her.' His harshly riven features turned his face into planes and angles. He would have been handsome if he weren't so tough-looking. Frown-lines were gouged in his brow, deep slashes from his hawk-like nose to a grim mouth that defied any sort of description. 'And why aren't you wearing a hat?'

The full intensity of his censuring blue eyes seared painfully through Caron as she faced him. His powerfully muscled body was clad in close-fitting cords and a check shirt, sleeves rolled back to reveal sinewy arms and bulging biceps.

She felt disinclined to tell him that it had been a moment of impetuosity that had made her jump on the horse and ride bare-back across the moor. It had been an exhilarating, thrilling ride, she had felt at one with the animal, until Sandy, named after the colour of her coat, had reared for no apparent reason and then charged as though all the hounds in hell were after her. Unable to stop her headlong flight, Caron had concentrated all her attention in hanging on.

'What I do is my business,' she declared aloofly, knowing she ought to thank him for stopping the horse but finding it difficult to be gracious when he was so obviously angry. What on earth was wrong with the man that he behaved like this?

'Have you far to go? Do you intend riding the horse back?'

Or had she lost her nerve? It was a third, unspoken question and Caron felt a prickle of annoyance. 'Of course I shall ride her back.' What did he think she was going to do, walk?

'She needs rubbing down, and soon, or she'll catch cold,' he told her crisply. 'You'd best go now. Do you make a habit of riding without a saddle? It's a very dangerous practice and it's a wonder it hasn't made you sore.'

'I like to feel the horse beneath me,' Caron retorted at once. 'Come on, girl.' She patted the horse and looked around for a suitable boulder or tree-stump. Normally she would have taken a running leap and hauled herself up, but she felt such an action would be too undignified in this man's presence.

Without a word the stranger linked his hands to form a stirrup and also without speaking Caron stepped on to them and swung her other leg over the horse's back.

'Maybe I should come with you?' His tone was deep and gruff and only slightly less fierce, and his eyes still blazed with a very real anger. 'I don't like to think that this beautiful mare might take fright again.'

Always the mare, never her, thought Caron bitterly. This man certainly did have a thing against women. 'It was a one-off thing, I'm sure,' she countered. 'You really have no need to worry.'

He nodded curtly, their eyes meeting for a few explosive seconds, until Caron pressed her knees into Sandy's sides and the horse moved obediently forward. 'Thank you for your help,' she called belatedly over her shoulder, catching a glimpse of him standing there, tall and forbidding, his blue eyes narrowed enigmatically.

She rode the mare sedately back to the stables, all the time her mind on the stranger. His attitude had been severe to say the least and yet there had been something about him, something in his compelling blue eyes, that made him difficult to forget. He was a charismatic man, the sort once seen, never forgotten.

By the time she got back the horse had cooled down but there were still traces of sweat on her body and John frowned as Caron rode into the yard, wanting to know why she had been riding his mare so hard. 'You ought to have more sense, Caron.'

'It wasn't my fault,' she defended hotly. 'Sandy took fright and bolted. I've no idea why, I didn't see a thing, but I certainly couldn't stop her. We went for miles and miles.' An exaggeration perhaps, but that's what it had felt like.

'Where were you exactly?' asked John thoughtfully.

Caron told him and he went quiet. 'What's wrong?' she asked. 'Do you know what happened?'

Her brother lifted his broad shoulders. 'It's a tale I've heard; I never really believed it, but maybe there is some truth in it after all. Over a hundred years ago a horse was supposedly shot on the moor and ever since has haunted the area, panicking any horse that happens to pass over the exact spot. You were lucky to be able to stop her. I've heard of horses running until they drop from sheer exhaustion.'

'I didn't stop her,' confessed Caron. 'A man appeared in the forest and hung on to her like grim death.' Maybe he was a ghost too!

'What man?' frowned John.

Caron shrugged. 'I've no idea. He didn't give me his name. He was very big and strong and had black curly hair and a surly face. You should have heard him tell me off. He said I shouldn't be riding if I couldn't handle the horse.'

Her brother suppressed a smile. 'I think I know who you mean. He lives in an old stone cottage on the edge of the woods. It used to be a holiday cottage, but hasn't been used for a long time. He hasn't been there very long and keeps himself very much to himself. No one knows anything about him. He's very much a mystery man.'

'They're not missing much,' scorned Caron. 'He actually seemed more concerned about Sandy than me.'

'He wasn't to know that you've been riding horses almost as long as you've been walking. Jump down and I'll get one of the lads to see to her. Go and rest for a while. You look very shaky yourself.'

Shaky wasn't the word, thought Caron, as she mounted the stairs to her room. She felt absolutely exhausted. But she wasn't sure whether it was because of her experience with the horse or meeting the mysterious stranger. She could not get him out of her mind. She kept seeing the fierce blue eyes in a savage face and a powerfully built body that had the strength of a horse, and it irritated her that he should have made such an impression. Since Karl she'd had no interest in other men.

Caron and John Lorimer looked nothing like brother and sister. She was small and blonde with dancing green eyes whereas he was tall and serious with dark brown hair and hazel eyes. He was the elder by five years and had bought this riding stable in Southern Ireland after the break-up of his marriage two years ago. A sprawling house went with it, an office added on at the back. There was a huge yard and purpose-built stables and tack-room, and beyond it the paddocks where the horses were kept most of the time.

Their parents had once owned a large farm in Dorset in England, and by far the best way of getting around it was on horseback. Caron was as skilled a rider as any man but she had never encountered anything as spooky as when Sandy took fright. It had scared her almost witless, though she would never have admitted it to the stranger.

When her father died suddenly Caron's mother sold the farm and moved to the Scilly Isles to live with her sister, and Caron moved to London, thinking it would be more exciting, but it hadn't worked out like that. She had trained as a secretary but had never really enjoyed the city and when the advertising company for whom she worked was taken over and she was made redundant she thought it an excellent opportunity to pay her brother a long-promised visit. She was even hoping he might find her a job.

She had been here for over two weeks now and as John had his full quota of staff there hadn't been very much for her to do, so when the next morning one of his stable-girls reported in sick Caron was delighted to help.

She was leading a string of novice riders when she saw him again, the man with the curly black hair! He was striding along, hands pushed deep in the pockets of his well-fitting corduroy pants, his face dark and broody. A hesitant smile curved her lips, but he refrained from even acknowledging her and strode straight past, back ramrod-straight.

It was very evident that he had intentionally ignored her, because in this country of warm-hearted people even strangers spoke. Caron felt a flare of anger at his rudeness, though his attitude did not surprise her after the way he had behaved yesterday. As her brother said, he was a man who liked to keep himself very much to himself.

Disturbingly, though, he refused to go out of her mind. Caron was the sort of girl who hated mysteries, who always needed to know the whys and wherefores of everything, and she knew that she would not be satisfied until she had found out what his name was and what he was doing here.

It had become her custom to go out for an early morning canter and the next day she deliberately chose a route very close to where she had met the man in the woods. Almost at once she saw him striding along, deep in thought. Caron slowed her horse at his side and he looked at her for an instant, then turned his head away without the slightest sign of recognition.

'Good morning,' she called with determined cheerfulness. 'Isn't it a lovely day?' She was not going to give up without a jolly good try.

But still he did not speak, marching onwards, telling her without words that he had no wish for her to be a part of his life, that he wanted her to go away and never speak to him again.

Caron kept pace with him for a few yards, knowing she ought to leave well alone, but still filled with an insatiable curiosity that she knew wouldn't easily leave her.

He wasn't as tall as she had first thought, probably just over six feet; it was the breadth of him, and the power he seemed to emanate, that had made him seem like a giant. He had a long, easy stride, almost a loping gait like an animal's and she could imagine muscles rippling beneath the casual clothes he wore so handsomely. Never in her life had she been so intrigued by a man.

'You'll be pleased to know that the mare's all right,' she called down. She wasn't on Sandy today, she was riding a chestnut gelding who obeyed her every command. 'She didn't suffer any ill effects.'

Still he ignored her and Caron knew she was wasting her time. Nevertheless she tried once more. 'My name's Caron, what's yours?'

Again a stony silence and in defeat she trotted the pony away, her head held high, resisting the urge to look back. Had she done so she would have seen the black-haired man looking after her, his blue eyes narrowed into an assessing frown.

Caron had a neat, dainty figure which belied a tomboyish trait. With her long, straight blonde hair, which she usually wore brushed back at the sides, the front falling into a soft fringe, she looked the sort of girl every man wished to protect. She had an almost porcelain complexion and rarely wore make-up, her green eyes were wide and thick-lashed, her nose flared slightly and her mouth was wide and generous.

For the rest of the day she determinedly pushed all thoughts of the stony-faced stranger from her mind. What was the point in filling her thoughts with a man who had made it abundantly clear that he wanted to be left alone?

When her brother asked her to fetch some provisions from the village store she was not even thinking about him, and it came as quite a shock to see the black-haired giant waiting in the queue to be served when she turned to leave the shop.

His expression was as saturnine as ever and he did not even see her! He saw no one. He went about with his eyes and mind shuttered to the outside world. He was like no one else she had ever met and Caron's determination to get through to him revived.

She lingered, studying the contents of the shelves, not moving until he was ready to go out of the shop, then seeing to it that they both reached the door at the same time.

Totally preoccupied with his thoughts, he was unaware of her until they collided. He looked at her sharply and recognition dawned in the piercing blue depths of his eyes, but with little more than a surly apology he strode on his way.

Caron hurried after him. 'Wait a moment. Can't we walk together?'

The look he threw her was one of complete intolerance and without a word he quickened his steps.

Although Caron felt hurt by his rebuff she was not ready to give up. 'Why won't you speak to me?'

He stopped so abruptly that she almost cannoned into him, and looked at her with eyes that were as cold and brilliant as diamonds. 'If there's something you want to say then get on with it.'

For a moment the harshness of his words stunned her and she gazed at him mutely. The she stuttered, 'I—I just thought—I felt—I wanted——' She was making a mess of it and the longer they stood there the more foolish she felt.

'I'm waiting.'

The abrasiveness of his voice grazed over her skin like a rasp and she shivered beneath the piercing intensity of razor-sharp eyes, eyes that saw everything but gave nothing away. Blue and fierce, hot one moment, cold the next, eyes that could strip defences with one sweeping glance. Eyes that could make love without a word or a touch!

Now why had she thought that? Her interest in him surely had nothing to do with sexual attraction. She had been hurt enough in the past not to want to get involved again. 'I was wondering why you live alone, that's all. Why you keep yourself to yourself. No one seems to know anything about you and I——'

If his eyes could have flailed her they would have. Caron almost reeled beneath the furious contempt that turned them to glittering ice. 'What I do is my own affair—and I plan to keep it that way. I'd thank you to keep your nose out of my business.'

Before she could utter another word he strode away. This time Caron did not follow and she was left feeling both devastated and humiliated. His harsh voice had cut through her like a knife. She ought never to have asked him such personal questions. She ought to have known he would take offence. She ought to have realised from their previous encounters that she was wasting her time. All she had done was made a fool of herself.

When she got home she told her brother what had happened. 'I'm not surprised,' he said with a reproving frown. 'You should have had more sense than to speak to him. Most people respect his wish to be left alone. One day you'll learn that you can't push your nose into everyone's business.'

And yet still the solitary man continued to intrigue her and Caron knew she wouldn't be satisfied until she found out why he had chosen to live by himself in a bleak stone cottage in the depths of the Irish countryside.

Out riding several days later Caron urged her horse over a thick hawthorne hedge, feeling wonderfully, totally exhilarated, laughing out aloud with sheer enjoyment. However her laughter turned into a startled cry when her mount landed awkwardly in an overgrown ditch and she was pitched forward over the animal's head.

She remembered landing, slamming against the ground, every ounce of breath knocked out of her, but she was aware of nothing more until she felt a man's hand on her leg, moving slowly and surely up from her ankle to her thigh. Her eyes shot wide—and met ice-blue! She struggled to sit up. 'What do you think you're doing?' she asked indignantly. 'How dare you? Let me go this instant!'

'Lie down and keep still.' A firm hand on her shoulder effectively immobilised her, and the harsh abrasion in his voice made it clear there was no sexual motivation behind his actions. 'I'm feeling for broken bones.'

If Caron had been thinking rationally she would have known what he was doing but in that instant her thoughts were far from lucid, though she wasn't sure whether it

was the shock of the fall or the shock of finding this
man touching her that was the cause of it.

His expert fingers moved to her other leg and then to
her arms while she lay and looked at the intent expression on his hard-boned face. There was a faint grey
line around the blue of his eyes, giving them added em-
phasis, and his thick eyebrows grew up straight where
they reached the bridge of his aquiline nose. It was definitely a strong face, with interesting lines that told of a
life that had not been easy.

When they weren't compressed into a grim line his lips
were much fuller than she had first imagined; sensual
lips, she decided, and unbidden came the thought that
she would like to be kissed by him. She dashed it away
instantly and angrily. She had firmly vowed after
breaking her engagement that she would never get involved with another man, not for a long, long time
anyway. He would have to be someone really special
before she was prepared to trust him.

'You don't appear to have injured yourself,' the man
said tersely. 'Sit up and tell me if anywhere hurts.' His
long fingers probed her ribcage and were far too near
her breasts for comfort. But it was clear by his dark expression that he was deriving no physical gratification,
that his actions were purely clinical, and for this Caron
was thankful.

Caron had actually never met a man who was immune
to the opposite sex and she wondered whether he had
suffered a similar bad experience to herself? He was
without a doubt a most virile-looking male and it didn't
seem natural that he should treat her with so much contempt. She felt sure she didn't deserve it.

'You're lucky,' he claimed at length, 'but I suggest
you come back to my cottage and lie down until you've

completely recovered.' The offer was made with barely contained reluctance.

'I'm sure that's not necessary,' said Caron sharply, wanting to go with him because here was the chance she had been seeking to find out more about him, and yet afraid at the same time. 'I feel perfectly all right.' She did not know the first thing about him, not even his name, and for all his apparent uninterest he might have been waiting for just such a moment!

'I insist,' he said grimly, and before she could even anticipate what he was going to do Caron found herself lifted by arms as strong as wire hawsers, held against a chest as solid as a plank of wood—except that it lived and breathed and was warm and vital!

His heart beat steadily, neither the exertion of carrying her, nor the feel of her perfumed body next to his affected his breathing. He was completely immune to her and she knew she was going to be safe.

On the contrary, much to her disgust, her own body responded of its own volition to his aggressive masculinity. The clean, fresh, outdoor smell of him assailed her nostrils like a drug, and there was an exciting warmth to his body that annoyingly quickened her pulses. How could such a thing be happening to her?

He did not put her down until they were inside the austere, single-storeyed grey stone building on the edge of the forest. The cottage amazed her by its smallness, though its stark appearance suited him perfectly. With a gentleness that was surprising he laid her on a blanket-covered couch and stood looking at her for a long, tension-packed moment.

Caron wished she knew what thoughts were going through his mind. His face as always was totally blank, although his jaw was tense, and she guessed he was dis-

pleased by the fact that he had felt compelled to help
her.

'Lie there and get your strength back,' he commanded
tersely. 'Meanwhile I'll go and look for your horse.
Getting into trouble seems to be a habit of yours.'

'Please, you needn't bother, he'll probably——'

Her words were wasted, he had already gone. Caron
knew it would be a futile exercise because the horse would
undoubtedly make its way back to the stable. Every one
of John's horses had this homing instinct. On the plus
side, though, it would give her the opportunity to have
a look at the place this strange man had chosen to live
in. Perhaps her accident had been a blessing in disguise.

She sat up and gazed about her. It was definitely not
a homely cottage. The dresser and table were solid and
old without being of any real value, the couch was lumpy,
and although it was a sunny day the room was in shadow
and distinctly chilly. What a world of difference a
crackling log fire would make, she thought, rubbing her
arms. It might even make the man more human! Then
she remembered they had peat fires in Ireland and she
had no idea whether they blazed as cheerfully as logs.

With great daring she crossed the floor and pushed
open a door in the corner. A tiny old-fashioned kitchen
with a stone sink and very few cupboards met her eyes.
It looked as though no one ever used it; in fact neither
of the rooms looked lived in. She found it very strange.

Another door revealed a bedroom, cramped by an
enormous bed, a sturdy oak wardrobe and a set of
drawers. Again it looked unused and, consumed by curiosity, Caron peeped into the wardrobe. She half expected to find it empty but instead saw a regimented row
of neatly pressed shirts and trousers and suits. But they
told her nothing about him except that he liked ex-

pensive clothes and had a tidy mind. What a mystery this man was.

Tentatively she opened a drawer, her heart thudding because she knew she was in the wrong, but curiosity overcoming fear. Before she could even glance at the contents a firm hand clamped her shoulder.

'What the hell do you think you're doing?' The man's tone was brutally caustic and scraped over her skin like steel wool. He moved amazingly quietly for so big a man, she thought, and as he spun her to face him she saw that he was more violently angry than ever before, eyes glittering flames of blue light, nostrils dilated, jaw taut. 'Why were you prying? What did you expect to find?'

He gripped her upper arms now and each sentence was accompanied by a threatening tightening of those long, hard-boned fingers. Tomorrow there would be telltale bruises and there was no one she could blame but herself. Whatever had possessed her to pry?

When she did not answer, when she continued to look at him in wide-eyed embarrassment, he shook her as if she were a rag doll. 'What are you,' he snarled, 'a private investigator? Or just plain nosy? Tell me, what have you found out?'

'Nothing,' she whispered at length. 'I don't know what came over me. I——'

'You don't know what came over you?' he sneered. 'You don't know? When you've done nothing but show interest in me ever since that first unfortunate meeting?' White teeth gleamed in the shadowy depths of the room, cold eyes pierced her, and when his hands slid over her shoulders to encircle the slender column of her throat Caron felt real fear.

'Unless it's my body you're really after? Is that it? Is your so-called interest a camouflage for much more basic needs?' His eyes narrowed as his face pushed close to hers. She could feel his warm, clean breath on her cheeks. 'I can think of no other reason why you constantly chase after me, and if that's the case perhaps I ought to oblige.'

Arms like whipcord suddenly bound her to him, her breasts crushed against a rock-hard chest, her lips claimed with harsh impatience, his tongue probing the trembling depths of her mouth.

With a fierce cry she pushed her hands against him and struggled to free herself. His bark of laughter held no humour. 'Afraid you've bitten off more than you can chew?' he derided with scorn. 'Let me give you a word of advice, young lady: never chase after a man you know nothing about.'

Caron's chin came up indignantly. 'I have no interest in you or any other man.'

Black brows rose disbelievingly. 'Can you deny that you have deliberately tried to engage me in conversation on more than one occasion?'

'Because you intrigue me, nothing more,' she returned with a defiant shrug of her shoulders. 'I certainly wasn't after your body. You must surely know that half the village is speculating on your presence here.'

'Then let them speculate,' he snorted. 'What I do is my own affair. And if you know what's best for you you'll get out of here now and stay out.'

'With pleasure,' she hissed through gritted teeth. 'If I never see you again I'll be happy.' With her head held high she walked out of the cottage.

He had not, as she suspected, managed to find the horse she had been riding, and because she had bruised her leg when falling she was daunted by the thought of having to walk back to the stables. But he did not offer her a lift and she was determined not to ask.

She felt him watching her as she limped along the well-beaten track through the woods. What a swine he is, she thought, what a brute of a man. How dared he try to take advantage of her? She felt quite sure that he had deliberately misinterpreted her actions, that he had derived some sort of sick pleasure out of kissing her, and if that was the type of man he was then she certainly wanted nothing more to do with him.

John met her as she limped the last few yards, a worried frown on his brow. 'I've been told Danny came home over an hour ago. What happened?'

'I fell off,' she admitted shamefacedly.

'That much I gathered. Where have you been all this time? I've only just got in and was about to come looking for you.'

Caron grimaced wryly. 'My black-haired friend's been looking after me.' Her tone was curt, making it clear she wanted no further questions asked.

John frowned. 'So where is he now? Why has he let you walk home in this condition?'

Caron shrugged. 'It was my decision. I'll go and take a bath, if you don't mind.'

Her brother frowned after her as she walked into the house but how could she tell him what had happened? He would say it was her own fault, that she had brought it on herself by openly showing her interest. And he was probably right. If she had contained her curiosity nothing would have happened.

Several more days went by, during which Caron tried to push all thoughts of the dark stranger out of her mind. She made herself concentrate on the work she was doing for John—he still had a staff shortage and there was plenty to do.

CHAPTER TWO

THE stranger was talking to John and it was too late for Caron to retreat. His cold blue eyes flickered mercilessly over her tight-fitting jeans and thin cotton top, probably recalling with perverted pleasure the day his hands had explored her body, her mouth vulnerable beneath his. A curt greeting was forced by good manners from his lips, but it was obvious that he was as surprised and as dismayed to see her as she was him.

John put his arm about his sister's shoulders and said to the man at his side, 'I think you two have already met? In fact, Lawson, I believe I owe you my thanks for looking after Caron the day she was thrown from her horse?'

'I only did what any man would have done,' said the black-haired stranger, eyeing her unsympathetically.

Did he mean any man would have touched her the way he had? mused Caron crossly.

'Lawson Savage feels like doing some riding,' explained John. 'I'm lending him Hunter. Will you take him over to the paddock?'

Savage! The name suited him perfectly, but accompanying him to the paddock was the last thing Caron wanted. 'I was just about to saddle up Rosemarie,' she demurred. 'Jane will be here for her lesson any minute.'

'Jane can saddle up herself,' John pointed out, frowning at the stubbornness in her tone.

Begrudgingly she led the way to the field, her skin prickling as she felt the big man watching her. Her body-hugging jeans revealed every curve and the pink cotton top under which she wore no bra was not much better. She was understandably proud of her trim figure but she did not like the thought of this man's eyes on her. Especially not after his brutal kiss.

As she made to open the gate his hand came down on hers, warm, firm, long-fingered and strong, the back covered with wiry dark hairs. She found herself wondering whether his chest was equally as hairy and then dismissed the thought as unworthy. She did not want to know these things. She did not want anything to do with him.

'Does dear John know that you've been chasing after me?' he asked curtly, blue eyes slicing through her with the swift thoroughness of a steel blade.

It took Caron a few seconds to realise that he was under the impression that John was her boyfriend, and she laughed, a high-pitched, nervous sound, nothing at all like her usual contagious giggle. 'You're mistaken; John's——'

'No, I don't suppose he does know,' he cut in swiftly and viciously, giving her no opportunity at all to finish her sentence. 'Boyfriends and husbands are usually the last ones to find out anything like that.'

His tone was so bitter that Caron wondered whether he was speaking from personal experience. Was that why he was here? Was he married? Had his wife two-timed him? Was this the problem?

Caron snatched her hand away and wished he would move so that she could open the gate. No matter what her feelings were towards this man she was beginning to find it impossible to dismiss his overt sexuality. And all because of one kiss! What a crazy situation she was finding herself in.

'But you're a pretty young thing without a doubt,' he continued, eyes narrowed as he looked her over insolently. 'I think perhaps I've been celibate long enough.'

'You keep away from me,' cried Caron in horror as his intentions became clear.

'Scared your boyfriend might find out?' he taunted. 'Changed your mind, have you? Stopped chasing me? Afraid you've bitten off more than you can chew?' His hand clamped her wrist again and he yanked her close. Caron's heart clamoured. There was a hardness to his eyes that was scaring. He was no longer an intriguing stranger, but a frightening, threatening man.

'You women are all the same,' he growled. 'Never content with one man, always needing the excitement of an illicit affair, not caring who you hurt in the process.' His lip curled in a derisive sneer. 'Oh, yes, I've been hurt, hurt enough to want to shut myself away forever, but I'm only human, and you—you've aroused the blood in my veins, and I don't see why I shouldn't take what you've been freely offering.'

Caron swallowed a lump the size of a golf ball in her throat and tried in vain to pull herself free. Fear ran like quicksilver through her limbs. He meant every word and the sooner she got away from him the better.

But the more she struggled, the tighter he held her, pulling her body close against his. 'God, you have the power to drive a man crazy,' he muttered thickly.

'You touch me and I'll——' Caron got no further; his mouth closed over hers and for a fraction of a second, before instinct to fight took over, mind-shattering desire pulsed through her veins. But it was a short-lived emotion. Even before she began to protest he let her go as abruptly as he had taken her.

'I guess now is neither the time nor the place,' he grunted. 'I will save the pleasure.' The blue light in his eyes sent a shiver down her spine. His words were a threat not to be taken lightly. And yet—contrary to everything she knew she ought to feel and fear—her body had responded to his.

Her throat still choked with emotion, she pointed out Hunter and turned and fled. His derisive laughter followed. Did he know? Had he sensed her reaction even in that brief moment? Colour flamed her throat and cheeks. She hoped she hadn't given herself away. It was an insane thing to have done in the circumstances.

He seemed to be under the impression that she had chased after him with one thing only in mind. How wrong could he be, and why hadn't she corrected him? Why had she let him go on thinking it? What an idiot she was.

When she got back to the yard Caron was relieved that John was nowhere in sight. The last thing she wanted was a discussion about Lawson Savage.

For the next few days she kept herself determinedly busy around the stables, going out on no more early morning rides, or indeed at any time of day, determined to avoid at all costs a further confrontation with Lawson.

The weather was mixed, quite often raining, a soft, gentle rain that was actually quite pleasant to be out in. It was this frequent rain that made Ireland the verdant country it was. One day, however, the sun shone gloriously, and, taking advantage of it, Caron sat out in John's small square of garden. She was happily listening to sparrows squabbling and blackbirds singing, inhaling the heady scent of honeysuckle and roses, when she heard the clip-clop of hoofs in the lane that ran alongside the house—and across the rhododendron hedge she encountered the glittering blue eyes of Lawson Savage.

'I've returned Hunter,' he explained needlessly.

His tone was impersonal though his eyes seemed to peel a layer off her skin as they made a slow and thorough appraisal. Caron wore a short cotton sundress and she had hitched the skirt up even higher to try to tan her bare legs. It was the first time this man had seen her in anything other than jeans and the longer he looked at her, the more uncomfortable she felt. She was tempted to smooth down her skirt but knew the action would give away her unease.

'You'd better take him down to the paddock,' she said tautly and, opening a magazine, pretended an interest she was far from feeling. It angered her that her heart-beats quickened when she had no real interest in him—or any other man for that matter. The way Karl had treated her had put her off men for a very long time—so why the unhealthy response to this man? It wasn't even as if he were attracted to her. It was hate at first sight for both of them.

'I haven't seen you around lately.'

Compelled to look at him again, Caron felt a warmth crawling over her skin and when he dismounted, tying Hunter loosely to the gatepost before walking across to her, she gave a silent groan.

'Have you been avoiding me?'

'Why should I do that?' Her chin came up with characteristic defensiveness, her green eyes challenging. He towered above her, long, powerful legs encased in blue denim, hips narrow, stomach hard and flat, a black T-shirt stretched tautly across his muscular chest.

'Perhaps because you're afraid?' he jeered, his eyes never wavering from hers.

'Of you?' she countered coldly, springing to her feet, hating the way he had the advantage. 'I don't think so, Mr Savage.' And she still had to look up at him, the top of her head barely reaching his shoulders.

He frowned at her use of his surname. 'Then afraid of yourself, perhaps? I know perfectly well that your body responds to mine the instant I touch you, but I'm not foolish enough to think that I'm different from any other man you set your sights on. However, I'm prepared to wait for my pleasure. You can't hide away from me forever. Where's your boyfriend?'

So he *had* sensed her response! Any faint hope Caron had sustained was dashed. 'John's out,' she told him coldly, 'and for the record he's not my boyfriend, he's my brother.'

Black brows rose. 'Your brother, eh? Now that does surprise me. Why the subterfuge, I wonder?'

'There was no pretence,' she defended. 'You assumed he was my boyfriend and never gave me the chance to deny it.'

'Does he know what you're like?' he barked.

'What do you mean, does he know what I'm like?' countered Caron with an angry frown. 'I haven't done anything.'

'No?' Still the bushy black brows were riding high. 'Do you consider prying into my drawers and cupboards nothing? Do you consider pursuing me, when I'd made it very clear I wanted to be left alone, nothing?'

Caron looked at him scornfully. 'I was not and still am not interested in you in the slightest—not in the way you're suggesting. You simply intrigued me, and I've already told you that so why don't you believe it? I unfortunately happen to have a highly inquisitive nature. It was a mistake trying to talk to you, and one I deeply regret, so perhaps now you know I'm not the type of girl you think you'll leave me alone.'

'That might not be so easy.'

'Why not?' she asked with a sudden frown.

'Because, Caron Lorimer, you're like a thorn deep under my skin, a thorn which hurts like hell but is difficult, if not impossible, to dig out.' His eyes glittered savagely and threateningly into hers. 'One day, one day soon, when the right moment presents itself, you and I will become lovers. Take my word for it. For the moment, however, I'll leave you to your sunbathing. Give my thanks to your brother.'

He strode arrogantly back to the patient horse, not mounting again but leading him down the lane without a backward glance, almost as though he had forgotten her already.

It angered Caron that this solitary man was able to get through the defensive wall she had built after Karl had abused her and she renewed her determination to never, ever give him the opportunity to get close enough to become her lover. No man was going to be her lover— not until she had a wedding-ring on her finger.

Oddly enough, though, when she saw nothing more of Lawson for several days Caron felt cheated, and even her brother asked her what was wrong. 'You've got a face as long as a wet week. Is something bothering you? Would it have anything to do with Lawson Savage, by any chance?'

Caron threw him a look of disgust. 'That man? He's the last person I'd let bother me. He's too pompous for words.'

'You were intrigued by him once.'

'Not any more, not now I've got to know him,' she snapped disparagingly. 'I don't like him at all.'

'That's a pity because he certainly seems interested in you,' said John, a smile tugging at the corners of his mouth.

Her head jerked and her eyes widened questioningly. 'In what way?'

'He asked me how old you were, whether this is your permanent home or whether you're visiting, whether you have a boyfriend. I'd say he's very keen on you.'

Keen on her! He was simply being careful before he laid hands on her. He didn't want any irate boyfriend baying for his blood. 'He's wasting his time,' she snapped.

'Is all this because of Karl?' her brother asked, suddenly serious. 'Don't you think it's time you started dating again?'

'Not with someone like Lawson Savage.' Her tone was sharp, telling him clearly that she did not want to pursue the conversation.

'I'm going to a horse sale tomorrow,' John announced, taking the hint and changing the subject. 'How about coming with me? It might cheer you up.'

'I'm not unhappy,' she protested, 'but yes, I'd love to come.' She did not want to take the risk that Lawson might call again when she was on her own.

The narrow, winding lanes were quiet and John drove his old Ford and horse trailer carefully, but neither of them could have anticipated the speeding sports car coming in the opposite direction, a car which took the bend far too wide.

Caron cried out, instinctively put her hands over her face, and waited for the moment of impact. John stamped on his brakes and wrenched the steering-wheel but with the trailer adding weight to the car his evasive action wasn't enough.

The silence that followed the collision was soul-destroying. Caron knew she was lucky to be alive and thankfully did not appear to be hurt even though the car was crunched in around her. John's side of the car had taken the brunt of the impact. John! She turned her head and saw him lying there twisted and deathly still, and she went ice-cold all over and felt violently sick.

Caron was dismissed from the hospital the next day, as was the driver of the sports car. They had both miraculously escaped with nothing more than cuts and bruises. The police had interviewed them both and the youth was being charged with reckless driving. But it was John's life that hung in the balance. His injuries were extensive and serious and no one could tell her how long he would be in hospital.

Thankful that she had learned something about how her brother ran the riding school, Caron was able, with the help of the rest of the staff, to keep it going. It would have been too awful to contemplate if everything John had worked for came to a halt because he was ill. It was the time of year when he was busiest. He needed to make enough money now to keep him going through the winter months when there were no holiday-makers and only local children wanting to learn to ride.

She had little or no time to think about Lawson Savage and he was the last person she expected to see when he turned up at the stables one day as she was on the point of leaving for the hospital.

'Going somewhere?' he asked tersely, eyeing her up and down in her smart summer dress.

Caron tossed her blonde hair off her face and looked at him with what she hoped was distaste, even though her pulses fluttered as though they were trapped butterflies. 'You haven't heard about the accident?'

Black brows drew abruptly together. 'What accident?'

'John's in hospital,' she told him bluntly, 'and I've been told I'm lucky to have escaped with no injuries myself.'

'A car crash?' he asked sharply.

She nodded.

'How did it happen?'

'We hit a sports car. The driver seemed to think he had the road to himself. We didn't stand a chance of avoiding him—or he us.'

'I'd no idea. How badly is John hurt?'

'Cracked ribs, a broken leg. So many cuts and bruises, you can't imagine it. They even suspected a fractured skull but that turned out to be a false alarm.'

'I'll come with you,' he said at once.

Caron gave an inward groan. This was the last thing she wanted, but without being rude how could she object?

For her daily journeys to and from the hospital she had hired a car, but before she could get into it Lawson plucked the keys out of her hand. She glanced at him angrily and began to protest, but then changed her mind. It wasn't worth arguing; he would probably make her nervous anyway, even though she prided herself on being a good driver.

'So what's happening to the riding school?' he asked, pushing the seat backwards to accommodate his long legs. 'Who's looking after it?'

'I am,' she told him coolly.

He glanced at her, his brows raised quizzically. 'You're expert at that sort of thing?'

Damn the man, he knew she wasn't. 'I'm managing,' she told him coldly. It was suffocating sitting next to him. He filled the car with his presence. She had never before met a man who wore his sexuality like a second skin. It could not be ignored, no matter how much she tried.

She was grateful that the journey took no more than a few minutes, but she was less than pleased half an hour later when her brother—who had been delighted to see Lawson walk in with her—asked him whether he would give her a hand in running things. 'Caron's doing her best but I'm sure she must be a bit out of her depth. Perhaps if she looks after the paperwork you can see that everything else runs smoothly. What do you think?'

Caron was ready to spit fire. How dared John offer Lawson a job without consulting her? And yet she knew it would be unwise to argue with her brother in his condition. He still looked desperately ill and shouldn't be worrying about work at all. But the thought of spending each and every day in Lawson's company was crucifying.

Lawson, on the other hand, looked extremely pleased with the arrangement. 'I must admit I hadn't planned to work while I was here, but if I can help out in any way at all I'll be only too pleased. I'm sure Caron and I will get on famously.' His eyes looked into hers as he spoke, a challenge in their steel-blue depths.

There was silence in the car as Lawson drove back from the hospital. Caron could not get over the fact that her brother had asked this man to help out. How did he know Lawson was capable? How did he know she wasn't managing as well as she'd hoped? Had someone been telling tales?

Admittedly there was more work to do than she had imagined. She had muddled a few bookings and some people had been given horses to ride that weren't quite suitable to their temperament, but when she'd explained about John they had all understood. Nothing serious had happened, there had been no accidents, so why was John insisting that Lawson give a hand?

Unless he was deliberately throwing them together? Was that it? Did he think she might revise her opinion of Lawson if she got to know him better? Had he no idea that this man was probably married?

'You're very quiet.' An amused smile curved Lawson's angular mouth as he glanced at her. 'Do I take it you're not happy with your brother's suggestion?'

Caron eyed him stonily. 'You're dead right I'm not. It's a stupid arrangement. You know even less about running a riding school than I do.'

'I'm a quick learner,' he said, trying to disguise a smile. 'And I think I shall enjoy it. Having you around will also make it that little bit more interesting, or should I say challenging?'

'Is that how you see me, as a challenge?' asked Caron, her head high, green eyes frosty.

'Oh, no,' he told her lightly, 'not a challenge in that respect. You offer yourself too freely.'

Caron's chin shot up. 'You swine! You dare lay one finger on me and I'll make sure you regret it.'

His eyes gleamed. 'What a little spitfire you are when you get going. But rest assured that I shall never force myself on you. There's no fun in that.'

'In that case,' she told him bluntly, 'you'll wait forever. I'm not interested in sex, with you or any other man.'

'John told me you'd had a bad experience.'

Caron swore softly beneath her breath. 'He had no right,' she snapped. 'But since you do know, yes, I did, and it would appear to make us two for a pair. Your opinion of women is much the same as mine is of men. I don't trust anyone any more, and I have no wish at all to associate with you. Do I make myself clear?'

'Absolutely,' he agreed, his face expressionless. 'But I imagine you, as much as I, sometimes feel a need to satisfy perfectly normal bodily urges?'

Caron gasped, feeling her cheeks flush an embarrassed red. What sort of a sick mind had he got to deliberately humiliate her like this? 'You're wrong,' she cried, 'sex is something I'm definitely not interested in.'

An eyebrow rose. 'Can you explain, then, why you feel aroused when I kiss you? If you're as anti-men as you suggest, you'd feel nothing except revulsion.'

Caron had been totally confused herself by her reaction, but she did not want this man pointing it out to her. 'You're mistaken,' she snapped, 'and I refuse to talk about it. It's a pointless conversation.'

'But interesting all the same.' He smiled in wry amusement. 'Nevertheless it's your prerogative. I'll concede to your wishes—for the moment.'

As he pulled up outside the house Caron glared at him coldly. 'I think it's best,' she said, 'that we keep out of each other's way as much as possible.'

Lawson reached across and touched the back of his hand fleetingly to her cheek, saying softly, 'Poor Caron. Will it be such a hardship?'

She was left with a burning sensation and an urge to strike out. But he had calculated his touch to perfection. Already he was out of the car and striding across the yard and in moments he had a circle of employees around him. They listened with intentness and deference to what he had to say and it was clear that he was a man used to handling people, and what was more they respected him.

Caron shook her head and marched angrily towards the house. It was good for her brother that Lawson was capable of running the business, but for herself she wished that he would fall flat on his face. He was too confident, too sure of himself, too everything! Damn the man! She wished they had never met.

'Caron—here a moment.'

Reluctantly she halted and turned and her eyes met his. The mocking humour was gone; this was a different side to Lawson. This was pure business. And if she had thought to defy him she changed her mind, crossing slowly to the little group of people.

'I've put everyone in the picture, Caron. Any complaints come straight to me. Anything to do with bookings goes to you. There's to be no slacking, by any of you, just because John's away. He's put me in charge and you'll find I'm a very fair man if you do your job well—if not, then you'd better look out.'

His eyes included her and Caron drew in a deep breath of resentment. As far as she was concerned they were equals in looking after this riding establishment. He was talking as though he were solely responsible. It was all she could do to hold her tongue and the instant he dismissed them she walked quickly back to the house. She had to get away from him before she said something she might later regret.

Again he called her back. This time she halted but did not turn, feeling the hairs rise on the back of her neck as he drew close. 'I need to know everything about the business,' he said. 'Now seems as good a time as any for you to explain.'

'Of course,' said Caron through gritted teeth, but the next hour was intolerable. Lawson stood much closer to her than was necessary, his arm constantly brushing hers,

and although his voice was kept businesslike she felt sure
it was a deliberate attempt on his part to arouse her. A
part of his diabolical plot to one day have her melting
in his arms and begging him to make love to her.

He would wait a very long time for that. She felt
nothing for him, nothing at all except a burning rage.
She blamed her brother for putting her in this pre-
dicament and the instant he was well enough she would
tell him so.

'Would you like a cup of coffee?' she asked at length,
needing to get away from him for a few minutes.

'Mmm, please—black, no sugar.' There was a gleam
in his eye as he answered, telling Caron all too clearly
that he knew exactly what he was doing to her.

In the kitchen she took a few steadying breaths before
filling the kettle and getting out cups. It was going to
be torture working with him every day. Please, John,
hurry up and get better, she prayed silently.

When she returned to the office Lawson was standing
at the window looking out across the yard. People had
arrived ready for their riding lesson and horses were being
saddled. It was a veritable hive of activity and as far as
Caron was concerned everything looked under control,
but Lawson turned, frowning. 'Is it always so chaotic?'

'I don't see anything wrong,' said Caron.

'It's mayhem out there. Nothing is properly organised. They don't know which horse they're supposed
to be riding. Everyone's going around in circles. Forget
the coffee, I fear I'm needed.'

They won't thank you for interfering, thought Caron
as he strode out of the house, but as she watched she
saw order created and realised that she had underesti-
mated him, unlike John, who had known instinctively
that this man would be able to take over, and what was

more handle everything as though it were a job he was used to.

She expected him to return to the house and was on tenterhooks for the next half-hour, watching from the office window, wondering where he was, feeling intense relief when she saw him leave the premises altogether.

She lay awake half the night thinking about him, worrying about the situation John had created, hoping, desperately hoping that Lawson Savage would keep out of her way.

Her prayers seemed to be answered the next day when he spent all morning outside and she was able to work on John's accounts and take telephone calls and bookings in relative peace.

She was in the kitchen making herself a cheese sandwich and a mug of coffee for her lunch when she heard him call her name. In seconds he had found her. 'Do you mind if I join you?'

'Yes, I do mind,' she told him coldly. 'I resent your making free use of this house.'

His eyes narrowed. 'As you weren't in the office and I heard sounds from the kitchen I calculated that this is where you would be. Can I share a sandwich?' His hand paused over the plate and she knew it would be churlish to refuse.

'Help yourself,' she shrugged. 'I'll make you some coffee, but this had better not become a habit. The office you can use, but the house is private property. No one comes in here without an invitation.'

'I'll remember,' he said, biting into the crusty bread with obvious relish, but Caron could tell from the amused expression on his face that he had no such intention of keeping away.

She cut him another two sandwiches, which he demolished with equal speed and satisfaction. 'There are things we need to discuss,' he said. 'How about over dinner tonight?'

'What sort of things?' she asked with a quick frown.

'To do with the riding school, of course. I have some ideas as to how it could be made to run more smoothly.'

'You can't do that,' she protested at once. 'You can't interfere in John's affairs.'

'I'm sure he won't mind,' said Lawson airily. 'But I intend going to the hospital this afternoon and speaking to him about it.'

'You're not to worry him,' insisted Caron. 'He's not up to it.'

Lawson smiled. 'Have no fear, my ideas will not disturb him; they're just simple little innovations, that's all. Why aren't you eating?'

'Because I'm suddenly not hungry,' she snapped.

'Then do you mind if I have this last sandwich?' He took a bite, watching her at the same time. 'You're very beautiful when you're angry, has anyone ever told you that?'

Caron eyed him stonily. 'There's only you who makes me angry. I didn't have a temper until I met you.'

'You mean I'm the only man to ever rub you up the wrong way?' His eyes widened disbelievingly. 'No one else has seen your eyes flash so magnificently? Or your cheeks burn so prettily? Not even this guy who upset you so much you ran away like a scared rabbit?'

'I did not run away,' she protested vehemently. 'It happened a long time ago. John was always asking me to visit him so when I was made redundant it seemed the ideal opportunity. That's why I'm here, not because I can't handle what happened to me.'

'So how long do you plan on staying?'

'I really have no idea,' she told him coolly. 'Now would you mind going?'

'Would you like to come to the hospital with me?'

Caron shook her head. 'I can't leave the office. I'll go when I finish here.'

'Then I'll pick you up at eight.'

'*If* I'm back,' she retorted coldly. 'I don't know why we need to discuss work over a meal. Why not here in the morning? It makes more sense.'

'Because, my dear Caron,' he answered with a wicked smile, 'I rather like the thought of your company. I'm getting a little tired of sitting by myself night after night.'

'You could go back home to wherever it is you come from,' she told him crossly. 'Haven't you a wife somewhere who must be worrying about you?'

At her words his face flushed a dark, angry red, and without answering her question he stood up and left the room.

CHAPTER THREE

SO THERE definitely was a wife somewhere, thought Caron, and, judging by Lawson's reaction to her angrily spoken words, it wasn't a happy marriage. He had walked out on her, perhaps? Or she had walked out on him? Whatever, he was still deeply disturbed, and she would be surprised if he hadn't brought it on himself.

His attitude was far too arrogant and high-handed for anyone ever to be happy living with him. He needed a subservient little mouse who did not mind being told what to do—and there weren't many girls like that about. Or else he needed someone as strong as he was. And would that really be a happy situation? Caron did not think so.

Ideally, Lawson needed a woman who could be as soft or as strong as each of his moods determined. She would need to be an intelligent and articulate companion, a good cook and hostess for when he entertained—he was obviously a businessman of some sort—but in bed she would have to be something else. Probably a complete wanton.

She had seen a brief glimpse of intense feelings the day he kissed her, knew what it would be like to be the recipient of such deep passion. But the woman he chose would also need to put up with his black moods—he was probably a workaholic as well and didn't spend as much time at home as he should. It all added up to his needing a very remarkable woman—and quite clearly his wife hadn't lived up to his expectations.

All afternoon she kept thinking about him, trying to imagine what sort of lifestyle he had left behind to become a virtual recluse in these quiet Irish backwoods. Whatever had happened between him and his wife, it had evidently hurt very much.

But shutting himself away and brooding had been the wrong thing to do. She had seen for herself the improvement since John had befriended him, and even more so now that her brother had asked him to help out with his business. He was a changed man.

At the hospital John looked a hundred times better. He was not in so much pain and his mind was easier now that he need no longer worry about the riding school. 'Lawson Savage is a blessing in disguise,' he said, as soon as she sat down on the chair at the side of his bed. 'He really has got a sharp business mind. How are you and he getting on?'

She grimaced, but, realising her brother was watching her face closely, turned it into a smile. 'It's too early to say.'

'Give him a chance, Caron,' he said softly. 'I don't know what grudge it is you've got against him, but he's not a bad sort. I have complete faith in him. He's made some suggestions to improve efficiency that are so simple, I can't think why I never thought of them myself.'

'I've no doubt he'll do the job well,' she returned sharply, 'and that's all that really matters, isn't it? What I think of him has nothing to do with it.' Or what Lawson thought of her!

A pretty young nurse paused by the bed. 'Is this your sister, John?' And when he nodded she went on, 'He's been telling me about some of the games you got up to when you were children.'

John smiled self-consciously. 'This is Liz, Caron. She's helping to make my life bearable.'

Caron looked from one to the other and thought she saw something more than a simple nurse-patient relationship. She was pleased for John. It would do him good to fall in love again after all the heartache he had suffered. His divorce had been pretty traumatic and he had come out here to bury himself in his work afterwards—much the same sort of thing as Lawson was doing. It made her wonder whether any marriages ever succeeded, and it made her all the more determined never to lose her heart to a man again.

It was half-past seven when Caron got home and she showered and dressed quickly for her dinner-date with Lawson. Her pretty pink sundress in a fine linen fabric was dressy enough for somewhere expensive but not over the top if they were eating in a less lavish establishment. She clipped mother-of-pearl earrings to her ears and wore white high-heeled, open-toed shoes.

It felt good to dress up and she even surprised herself by looking forward to the evening, and when Lawson knocked on the door she opened it with a smile of welcome on her face.

Lawson had always looked good in casual clothes, she had to acknowledge that, but in a slate-grey lounge suit with a white shirt and grey and gold silk tie he looked totally devastating, and there was nothing she could do to stop her heart quickening its beats.

His eyes flickered briefly yet thoroughly over her, but all he said was, 'I'm glad you're ready, let's go,' and she had no way of knowing whether the effort she had made was worthwhile. His car both surprised and impressed her. A silver-blue BMW, no less, and he made sure she was sitting comfortably before getting in himself.

She determinedly looked out of the window. The Irish countryside never ceased to please her. The greens and golds of the landscape were soft and muted because of the haze that hung in the air, and Caron had noticed before how, when a north-west wind blew and the clouds began to drift, shafts of changing light touched the land. Dorset was pretty but this was something different altogether. It had a rare beauty that the Irish were justifiably proud of.

But no matter how she tried it was impossible to concentrate completely on her surroundings and forget the man at her side. Lawson Savage was not a man anyone could easily forget—he had far too powerful a presence. But she was not going to let him disturb her. She had made a vow to herself that she would keep everything between them on a strictly business level.

Nevertheless when she glanced across at him their eyes met and a sudden warmth tingled her skin. She smiled briefly then looked away. It was going to be harder than she'd expected. He had a way of getting through to her whether she liked it or not.

'I thought John looked much better this afternoon.'

She was glad he had spoken about a safe subject, and nodded. 'Me too—and he seems to have his eye on one of the nurses. I'm pleased for him. He had a bad time when his marriage broke up.'

It was not until she saw a muscle go tense in Lawson's jaw that Caron realised she had said the wrong thing. 'I'm sorry, I'd forgotten you're going through a bad patch yourself.'

An abrupt frown furrowed his brow. 'What do you know about my affairs?' he asked harshly.

'Why, nothing,' she said at once. 'I'm simply—assuming.'

'Well, don't,' he snarled. 'That's where people get things wrong—by assuming. You know nothing about what's happened and I'd like it to stay that way.' His mouth was grim now, he was nothing like the relaxed man of a few seconds earlier.

'I'm sorry if I've aroused memories that are painful,' she said, 'but really I don't think I deserve to be shouted at. How was I to know you felt so strongly?'

'Goddammit, why are women so infernally nosy?' he rasped. 'Why can't they leave well alone? If you know what's good for you, Caron, you won't mention my past again. It's over, it's done with and I don't want reminding of it.'

'Excuse me for speaking,' she said angrily. 'Perhaps you'd like to turn around and take me home? It was your idea to eat out, don't forget; I wanted nothing to do with it.' She felt sure he was making a mountain out of a molehill. Her own past had been devastating enough but she wasn't letting it interfere with her life to such an extent that she went moody if anyone mentioned it.

'The table's booked,' he told her bluntly. 'I have no wish to change our plans.'

Caron shrugged. 'As you wish, but if I've got to watch what I say all evening it's not going to be very enjoyable.'

'There is only one taboo subject,' he told her sternly. 'If you keep off that we'll have no problem.'

For the rest of the journey they sat in silence, Lawson staring broodingly ahead, obviously dwelling on whatever it was that he was keeping secret from her, while Caron wished she had never agreed to come. It had been a mistake, a grave mistake, and the whole evening was turning into a disaster. Why didn't he end it now instead of prolonging the agony?

The restaurant was a whitewashed building that looked nothing more than a cottage. Inside two downstairs rooms had been knocked into one and were utterly charming with shamrock-green tablecloths and napkins, with brasses on the walls and crystal and silver on the tables. It was a dream of a place and Caron fell in love with it instantly. 'Why, it's lovely!' she exclaimed, looking about her in pleasure, instantly forgetting her anger.

'It has a good reputation,' Lawson agreed.

As there was no bar they sat at their table and their drinks were brought to them while they studied the menu. Lawson had an Irish whiskey, Caron white wine—she thought it safest not to have anything stronger.

All in all the evening passed far more pleasantly than she had expected. Lawson made a determined effort to be entertaining, pushing out of his mind everything that was bothering him. He drew her out to tell him about herself and her brother and the farm in Dorset, and her disastrous relationship with Karl.

'John didn't tell me exactly what happened between you and your fiancé. Why did you break up? Did you find some other man who appealed to you more?'

Caron flashed him a look of intense dislike. 'Trust you to think something like that. As a matter of fact it was Karl who two-timed me. I forgave him once but when it happened a second time, that was it.'

'You gave him his marching orders?'

'Which I should have done in the first place,' she retorted sharply. And what was she doing discussing her private life with this man who refused to tell her anything about himself?

When Karl Britt, a newcomer to the advertising company where she worked, had first asked her out she had been flattered and overwhelmed. He was exceedingly handsome and there were so many girls after him that she could not believe he had chosen her. Before long they began to go out regularly and eventually he had asked her to marry him.

Then she had overheard one of the other secretaries saying that she had seen Karl out with Gwynneth Browning. Gwynneth was a voluptuous redhead who had been after him for ages. When Caron had tackled him about it he'd assured her that all he had been doing was consoling Gwynneth because she'd had some bad luck.

Stupidly, blinded by her love, she had believed him, but then she had actually seen him herself out with another girl. She had been totally devastated but instead of losing her temper she had coolly and calmly handed him back his ring and told him that it was all over. 'You're free now to go out with whomever you like.'

It was not until she was back home in her flat that she had given way to the tears that had felt as though they were never going to stop coming. She had loved Karl so much, even letting him make love to her once they were engaged. She had very strong principles in that direction and had always sworn to remain a virgin until she got married. But he had been very insistent and she had thought that since they were going to get married it wasn't really like breaking her self-imposed vows.

After their break-up she had wondered whether the only reason he had asked her to marry him was so that he could make love to her. Right from the beginning it was what he had wanted. Had she been incredibly naïve, thinking that he loved her?

No one was more relieved than she when the redundancy notices were handed out. Karl was still with the company as far as she knew, still dating as many girls as cared to go out with him, earning himself quite a reputation. Caron herself had always maintained a discreet silence about their relationship.

Lawson had been watching her face as thoughts came and went, and now he said, 'So because of him you've decided to trust no other man?'

'I'd be a fool to,' she snapped.

Lawson in return told her absolutely nothing about himself. He talked about his plans for improving the way the riding school was run—nothing major: a change in the booking system, each employee having his or her own particular job instead of doing anything and everything and getting in each other's way, one or two other minor innovations. He refilled her wine glass frequently, he smiled often, but about his private life he remained silent.

It irritated Caron that he had persuaded her to open up while revealing nothing himself, but on the whole she was enjoying the evening much more than she had imagined. When Lawson put his mind to it he could be a very entertaining companion.

On the journey home, having drunk far more than she was used to, she felt pleasantly inebriated, and when Lawson stopped the car outside John's house she impulsively invited him in for a cup of coffee. She felt more happy and relaxed in his company than at any time since their explosive first meeting. He was proving to be not quite the ogre she had thought.

Her key was in the lock when she suddenly heard the screech of an owl and, turning quickly, she bumped into Lawson's hard body. His arm steadied her and an unexpected *frisson* of sensation ran like quicksilver through her veins. 'Did you hear that owl?' she asked, surprised to hear how breathless her voice sounded. 'They're my favourite bird. I haven't seen one since I left the farm.'

'I'm sure that can be remedied,' he said softly. Returning to his car, he produced a torch from beneath the seat, and they stood for a minute or two in total silence, shoulders touching, Caron's heart racing. When the owl screeched again from its perch in a lone tree Lawson pin-pointed it with his torch. For a few seconds the barn owl was hypnotised, his large eyes shining out of a round white face, and then he flew away, a ghostly white shape in the dark of the night.

'That was fantastic,' cried Caron, and, standing on tiptoe, impulsively kissed Lawson on the cheek. 'Thank you, I'm glad you had that torch.'

The next second her slender body was crushed against the hardness of his, his mouth swooping down to claim hers, and the instant their lips met every vow she had ever made was forgotten. He was as intoxicating as the wine she had drunk; his kiss was a rampant reminder of that time by the paddock gate when desire had flooded through her like a river out of control.

Belatedly she began to struggle, tried to clear her senses of him, realising she was making a fatal mistake. But it was too late, she had left it too late, he refused to let her go. He lifted his head long enough to examine her flushed skin and trembling mouth, to let her see the smouldering desire in his eyes, before with a groan he covered her lips again with his.

His hand moved beneath the heavy fall of her hair to caress the soft skin of her nape, slid slowly across her bare shoulders before descending to pull her even closer to him.

Caron suddenly found herself lost in a world of spinning senses, involuntarily threading her fingers through the thick coarseness of his hair, feeling the strong shape of his head. Her defences had fallen, she felt as though she was being consumed by an emotion far too intense to do anything about. She had felt nothing like this with Karl, even though she had been planning to marry him.

When Lawson suddenly and sharply drew away she looked at him in wide-eyed surprise. A sneer curved the fullness of his lips. 'I think I've proved for myself, Caron, that you're every bit the wanton you try to deny. In fact, I think I might just take you to bed and finish what you obviously want.' Even as he spoke he swung her up into his arms and carried her indoors.

Caron kicked and yelled and struggled. 'Let me go, you swine, put me down.' Whatever insane madness had made her respond, she was not going to let Lawson make love to her. Definitely not. One mistake in that direction was enough. Natural urges, that was what he had talked about the other day. She didn't have any of those. It was the drink that had done this to her; he had probably plied her with it deliberately, knowing the effect it would have.

She ought never to have gone along with the kiss. She ought never to have put herself in such a position. She ought to have stopped him at once. Why hadn't she? Why had she let him go on when she had known where it would lead?

He carried her upstairs, completely ignoring her protests, kicking open the first door he came to. Ironically, it was her own bedroom. He dropped her down on the bed and for an instant she stared at him in wide-eyed, mesmerised dismay, expecting him to tear off his clothes and bear down upon her. Instead he laughed, harsh, derisive laughter that chilled the blood in her veins.

'So you're the sort of girl who gets her kicks out of turning a man on and then backing off when the going gets too strong?' he sneered scornfully. 'I should have known.'

'That's not true,' she protested, pushing herself up and eyeing him angrily.

'Nevertheless, Caron,' he went on as though she had not spoken, 'I want you, and I mean to have you. Against my better judgement I'm attracted to you—it was there from the first moment we met. I've always been cynical about such things but obviously it does happen and I can't deny how I feel.'

'I'm not in the habit of letting *married* men make love to me,' she defended hotly, shocked and surprised by his confession, but knowing that all it meant was that he was as bad as Karl; he wanted to possess her body, he desired her, that was all. There were no actual emotions involved.

He drew in his breath in a savage hiss, every limb stiffening. His fingers flexed, his eyes glittered, and she pressed herself fearfully back against the pillow. But the next second he was out through the door and Caron was alone.

Again, mentioning his wife had aroused an incredible anger. He was so touchy about her, it was unbelievable, and Caron longed to know what had happened between them. But how was she ever going to find out when he clammed up whenever the woman was mentioned?

It had been a fatal mistake on her part, letting him see how easily he could arouse her, and how much she enjoyed his kisses. But it was done, and all she could do now was make sure that no opportunities ever arose for him to get close to her again. She did not believe that he was attracted to her. It was something he was making up in the hope that she would respond more easily to him. He was as bad as Karl in that direction.

After a restless night she got up early and took one of the horses for a gallop to clear her head. Back at the house she drank coffee but ate no breakfast, and was dreading the time when Lawson put in an appearance. He had told her that first thing each morning he intended coming to see what bookings had been made for the day. Perhaps if she left the office open but kept out of his way she'd manage to avoid him? But she dismissed the thought as cowardly. He had to be faced.

She worried for nothing. Lawson did not say a word about the previous evening. He was brisk and businesslike and entirely impersonal, which she found extremely puzzling after his declaration last night. On the other hand it helped her to treat him with similar detachment. Regardless, it was a long day and she was glad when it came to an end.

Several more days followed the same pattern. After his threat to make love to her Caron found it difficult to understand his attitude. They had begun to build a rapport on their night out, she was sure of it, and now they were back to square one again. Was it because she had responded and then backed off? Was he angry with her, disgusted with her? Did he think she was a tramp? The thought hurt. It hurt a lot, despite the fact that if he tried to touch her she would rebuff him again.

There were no weekends off in this job and Lawson seemed tireless but Caron yearned for some time to herself. She needed to escape this man's overpowering presence for at least a little while.

When she suggested to her brother that she would like a few days' holiday he was instantly agreeable. 'I don't expect you to work seven days a week with no respite.'

However, before she could mention it to the black-haired man who had again become her enemy her brother did it for her, and when Lawson came back from the hospital he looked far from pleased. 'I would have preferred you to tell *me* you wanted some free time. Your brother is really in no position to do anything about it.'

His sharp words stung but Caron held back swift retaliation and said instead, 'It's not healthy for anyone to work all the hours God gave.'

Blue eyes narrowed. 'Are you suggesting that I need time off too? That we should take it together?'

'Nothing of the sort,' she gasped. She had not dreamt that her words might be misconstrued. 'Spending time with you is the last thing I want.'

Black brows rose, blue eyes jeered. 'Backing off now, are we? You've finally realised that I prefer to be the hunter instead of the prey?'

'You're talking nonsense,' she snapped.

'Am I?' he demanded curtly. 'I don't think so. I'm trying to put things in their right perspective. And I think I have it about right. You still want me, isn't that so? And the fact that I've left you strictly alone for the last few days is driving you crazy? That's why you want some time off, isn't it? You want to get away from me.'

'You're demented,' she cried furiously, even as her cheeks blazed her guilt. But he was only half right. She did want to get away from him, yes, but not because of any longings for his body. That was the most ridiculous thing she had ever heard.

As she swung away he caught her wrist and pulled her roughly against him. There was no avoiding his descending mouth. 'Maybe I've been punishing myself too,' he grunted.

Caron struggled like a wild cat but it made no difference—the kiss went on and on, bruising, demanding, taking. Against her will she felt desire kick to life inside her but Lawson Savage was going to be the last person to know that. She resisted him with every ounce of her strength and when the office door opened and a red-faced stable boy stammered something before turning to race back across the yard she felt more relief than embarrassment.

Lawson's eyes blazed furiously into hers. 'This is something I definitely intend finishing another time; you don't fool me with your ice-maiden act. Maybe your idea of a break is not such a bad one after all. How about the weekend? We'll find somewhere deep in the countryside, somewhere where we won't be disturbed.'

'No!' Caron's eyes blazed a vivid green. 'I want time to myself. And besides, we couldn't both go away; someone has to look after things here.'

'I'll make sure that everything is properly organised,' he told her firmly. 'And yes, the more I think about it, the more I'm sure I shall enjoy your company. Now I'll go and see what that unfortunate boy wanted.'

Caron had no intention of going anywhere with Lawson Savage. He could not force her. He could not pick her up and carry her off.

It was while Lawson was at the hospital that same afternoon—he had taken to visiting John each day after lunch when all the horses were out and there was little to do—that a tap came on the office door. The girl who stood there had deep auburn hair and wide, troubled grey eyes. She was much taller than Caron, in her mid-twenties, and quite beautiful with a wide mouth and high cheekbones.

'I'm after Lawson Savage. I've been told that he's working here. I'd like to speak to him, please.' She had a husky, well-modulated voice.

'I'm afraid that's not possible,' Caron informed her. 'He's at the hospital. I——'

The girl's eyes widened in horrified dismay. 'Is he ill? Is something wrong? Oh, lord, tell me where he is; I must go to him.' She looked as though she was about to cry.

'No, no, nothing like that,' said Caron at once. 'He's visiting my brother, that's all. He'll be back later on. You can wait if you like.'

The instant relief that passed over the girl's face was like sunshine after rain. 'Oh, I'm glad. I mean, I'm sorry about your brother but I'm glad it's not Lawson. I'm Stephanie Savage and I——'

The name had barely sunk in before Lawson's footsteps were heard in the yard. The girl turned and with a cry of pleasure ran over to him. 'Oh, Lawson, thank God I've found you. I've been so worried—I've been searching for you everywhere.'

CHAPTER FOUR

CARON felt sickening, stinging jealousy as she slowly followed Stephanie Savage outside, jealousy which she had never expected, which she didn't want. She had sworn never to let herself feel for any man again and yet it had happened, completely against her will, and without her knowing it.

This had to be his wife, and whatever had caused their break-up there was no sign of it now on his face. He looked as pleased to see the girl as she was to see him, holding her close as though he never wanted to let her go again.

It was only belatedly that he seemed to remember Caron. 'Oh, Caron, this is Stephanie. Mrs Stephanie Savage, to be precise.' His eyes glinted mockingly into hers. 'Stephanie, Caron Lorimer.'

'Yes, we've met,' said Stephanie. 'Her poor brother's in hospital and I said I was glad. I'm so sorry, Caron. What's wrong with your brother? I hope it's nothing serious.'

'He'll be out in no time,' Caron smiled. 'We had a car accident. Nothing that he won't recover from——'

'How did you find me?' asked Lawson, impatiently cutting into their conversation.

'With a great deal of difficulty,' Stephanie answered sharply. 'Your brother and I looked everywhere and asked everyone, and then Bruce remembered how much you used to like coming to a cottage here when you were a boy. It was a long shot and you can't imagine my relief when they told me in the village that you were here. We need to talk, Lawson, can we go back to the cottage now? And I must let Bruce know that you're safe. He was as demented as me when you took off without a word.'

'You know why, Stephanie,' he told her quietly.

She nodded and looked as though she were about to cry.

Caron saw Lawson's Adam's apple go up and down as he swallowed hard. She found it difficult to take her eyes off both him and this girl who, whatever had gone wrong, was still clearly utterly devoted.

With a choking feeling in her heart she headed back to the office. From the window she saw them still talking urgently and quietly as they headed in the direction of the cottage in which Lawson had chosen to live.

The thought of them together turned her stomach into knots and she could not think how she had fallen in love with Lawson without being aware of it, but she had. It was an amazing discovery and not a welcome one. He had stormed her defences and brought her back to life and now his wife had turned up and by the look on his face it would not be long before they were reconciled. He would return to wherever it was he had come from and she, Caron, would be left nursing her wounds all over again. Why was she so vulnerable? Why had she let it happen? Damn the man. Damn, damn, *damn*!

Caron found it difficult to concentrate after that and was glad when the day came to an end so that she could lock up the office. But she could not help wondering what Lawson and Stephanie were doing—other than talking! She had expected him back at the yard when the horses were returned—he always liked to make sure that no one skimped in cleaning the tack or grooming

the patient animals. The sickness she had felt earlier
returned.

When the doorbell rang some minutes later she was
surprised to see Stephanie standing on the step. 'We'd
like you to come out to dinner with us,' she said at once.
Her face looked strained, nowhere near as happy as when
she'd first set eyes on Lawson. Their initial pleasure had
obviously been short-lived.

'I'm sorry, I'm going to the hospital,' said Caron,
wondering whether the invitation had been Stephanie's
idea. She could not believe that Lawson would suggest
it. Perhaps they'd had another argument and Stephanie
felt it would relieve some of their tension if Caron joined
them.

'We're not going until half-past seven,' insisted the
auburn-haired woman. 'I'd really like you to come.'

Caron nodded. 'Very well,' she agreed grudgingly.

At the hospital she told John that Lawson's wife had
turned up. 'It would appear that he up and left and told
no one where he was going. Everyone's been frantic with
worry.'

John looked thunderstruck. 'I didn't even know he
was married. He didn't tell you either?'

Caron shook her head. 'Though I guessed something
of the sort. And, whatever has happened between them,
it's obvious that Stephanie's still very much in love with
him.'

'I had hoped,' said her brother, 'that you and he would
resolve your differences and——'

'*John*!' she interrupted fiercely.

'I'm sorry,' he grunted. 'But if he's married there's
no chance of that now, is there? All I hope is that he
doesn't walk out and leave me in the lurch. Do you think
there's any chance of that?'

'I haven't the slightest idea,' she said, shaking her head. 'And by the way, I'm going away this weekend.' It had been worrying her so much, but now that Stephanie had turned up she would be able to go on her own after all. She would just drive and drive until she was tired and then book herself into a guest-house somewhere.

Caron had not been home long when Lawson and Stephanie came to pick her up. Lawson looked distinctly out of sorts, though Stephanie was doing her best to be cheerful. 'Lawson says he knows this little place that isn't much to look at but the food is superb. I love good food, don't you, Caron?'

Muttering some sort of assent, Caron climbed into the back of Stephanie's red Mercedes convertible. Lawson was in the driving seat and he took the corners as though they were in some sort of race. Even if he was angry, thought Caron apprehensively, he had no right to endanger their lives.

The restaurant lived up to its reputation, but none of them ate very much, toying with the food on their plates and making desultory conversation. Stephanie was doing her best to ignore Lawson's black mood but it was not easy when he was the sort of man who dominated any gathering. His mood rubbed off on them and they seemed to spend most of the time sitting without speaking.

'How long are you staying here, Stephanie?' asked Caron, after one particularly painful silence.

'I'm going back tomorrow,' she announced, much to Caron's surprise. 'I've spent enough time looking for Lawson. I must get back behind my desk before I'm sacked.'

Caron was amazed to hear that Stephanie was putting her job before her marriage. If that was the case why had she bothered to come here at all? Unless Lawson was going back with her?

'No, I'm not going,' he said, reading her face as clearly as if she had spoken her thoughts out aloud. 'I fully intend honouring my commitment to John.'

'I keep telling him he's got his priorities wrong,' grimaced Stephanie. 'He has his own business to run.'

To say nothing of their marriage, thought Caron.

'I've left it in good hands,' he growled.

'But you can't expect David to make the decisions forever,' persisted Stephanie. 'There must be times when he needs to consult you. At least let me tell him where you are.'

'*No!*' Lawson startled Caron by his ferocity. 'And I refuse to talk about it. Let's go.' He scraped back his chair and Stephanie and Caron were left to follow.

'I'm sorry about this,' said the auburn-haired girl. 'He really is a most impossible man when he gets a bee in his bonnet. Do you think you could have a word with him?'

'Me?' squeaked Caron. 'He won't listen to me.'

Stephanie frowned. 'I thought you and he had become good friends? He's spoken about you a lot.'

'He has?' To his wife! She almost choked.

'When I saw him this afternoon I thought what a difference there was in him—and it must have been all your doing, Caron. When he left home he was only a shadow of the man he used to be.'

Caron did not know what to say. 'He's changed, yes, I admit it, even in the short time I've known him, but it's not because of me, it's the work he's doing here. He really enjoys it.'

'You could be right,' admitted Stephanie reluctantly. 'He likes to be out of doors. Perhaps it's time he had a change.'

But would Stephanie enjoy a complete change of life-style? thought Caron when they were back in the car. It was possible that Lawson might like to go into part-nership with John, expand the riding school. Would his wife want to move? Caron shook her head and dis-missed her thoughts. Whatever he did, it was no business of hers. He was well and truly married and the sooner she put him out of her life and her mind the better.

Caron did not know exactly what time Stephanie was leaving but when Lawson turned up at the office at his usual hour the following morning she looked at him in surprise. 'Has your—er—Mrs Savage left already?' It was too painful to call her his wife.

'She left a few minutes ago,' he answered abruptly. 'Shall we get on? I believe we have a very hectic schedule today.'

His attitude was brusque to say the least; Stephanie's visit seemed to have done more harm than good. And at the end of the day she was shocked rigid when Lawson told her to be ready at eight the next morning.

Caron frowned. 'You're not serious?'

'Why shouldn't I be?'

'It's different now, with Stephanie coming and all that. I'm going away by myself as I originally planned.'

'Oh, no, you're not,' he barked. 'Nothing's changed. We're going together even if I have to use force.'

Caron felt an instant's fear, followed by a thrill of excitement. She knew he was perfectly capable of car-rying out his threat and she might as well give in with good grace, but what worried her most was the fact that she *wanted* to go with him! Despite the fact that he was married, despite the fact that she knew it would be a total disaster, not at all the sort of weekend she had envisaged for herself, she still wanted to go. It was crazy and yet that was the way it was. Her love took no account of wedding vows or previous destructive relationships. Everything fell before it, it marched blindly on and there was not a thing she could do to stop it.

She would have to hide her new-found love, of course, hide it completely. Letting Lawson see how she felt would be disastrous. Would it be possible to keep her feelings hidden in such circumstances? Would she have the strength and will-power to do it? What if she didn't? What if he found out? What would he say? Would he deride her or would he take advantage?

It was impossible to answer any of these questions and all she could do was go along with him and hope for the best. She heaved an exaggerated sigh. 'I seem to have little choice. Have you made any plans? Have you booked hotel rooms?'

'I think I'll let that be a surprise.' There was grim humour on his face as he spoke.

How she had managed to fall in love at all, Caron had no idea. It had crept up on her so unsuspectingly. He was the last man she had ever dreamt would get through to her and she did not want to be in love. She had already discovered to her cost that it was far too painful a process. She would have to fight it with every ounce of self-control.

On Saturday morning Caron was ready well before eight, having lain awake half the night wrestling with her problem. Lawson arrived five minutes early and it was clear by the grimness of his mouth and the blank expression in his eyes that he was still aggrieved in some way by Stephanie's visit. He glanced at her briefly. 'I'm glad you're ready.'

Caron felt she ought to suggest cancelling the weekend but knew he would jump down her throat if she did. He picked up her holdall, which stood just inside the door, and slung it into the boot of his car, then, taking the key from her hand, he locked the house and handed it back. It was not a very auspicious beginning, thought Caron.

However, despite his uncompromising behaviour she was still vitally aware of him. With every breath she drew she seemed to inhale part of him. Since her blinding flash of revelation when Stephanie had turned up she saw and felt everything so much more clearly and knew that his intention this weekend was to get her into his bed.

No man, at least no man of Lawson's virility, could live for long without a woman. He had admitted that once. And the way things were between him and Stephanie it would appear his thirst had in no way been slaked.

It would be difficult to say no, feeling as she did, but say no she must. If she dared let Lawson catch a glimpse of her feelings it would be the beginning of the end, yet another traumatic experience in her life. As things stood, while he was in ignorance, she could pretend her love did not exist.

She glanced across at his stony features and without thinking said, 'I can't understand why Stephanie's gone back without you.' The moment the words were out she regretted them.

His eyes narrowed and his tone was distinctly chilly. 'There was no reason for her to stay.'

No reason! There was every reason in the world. 'You mean you didn't want her here?' she accused. 'I don't understand you, Lawson Savage. What is it that you want in a woman? You won't find anyone better than Stephanie, and it's obvious she adores you.'

'Stephanie's one in a million,' he agreed, 'and yes, I suppose she is very fond of me—as I am of her.'

And yet he was letting her go, just like that, with a rift between them as wide as the English Channel. 'As far as I can see you're an out-and-out swine,' she snapped savagely. 'You don't deserve someone like Stephanie.'

His lips quirked and for a moment he actually looked amused. 'If you knew all the facts, Caron, you wouldn't say that.'

'Then why don't you tell me?' she suggested coldly.

'Because my private life is just that—private.' The snarl was back in his voice. 'And I'll thank you to keep your nose out of it. We're supposed to be relaxing and enjoying the countryside, not snipping and snapping and talking about something that does not concern you.'

Relax, when she was here under protest? It was the last thing she could do. The silence after that was painful. Frequently they paused to admire castle ruins or the patchwork pattern of golden cornfields and green meadows. Sometimes cows created traffic jams in the narrow country lanes and they would sit patiently until they moved. Lawson was in no hurry at all to get to wherever it was he was taking her.

Several times Caron found his eyes enquiringly on her, a deep, disturbing blue that sensitised her whole being until it was painful even to breathe. She wondered if he knew what he was doing. Whether he had somehow guessed the way she felt. Or did he see Stephanie instead of her? Were his thoughts still with this other girl?

They stopped for coffee and sandwiches at a roadside café and then pressed on further south. The countryside was in turn bleak and lonely, and lushly green. The heather-clad mountains dominated and they drove through a tunnel cut through the mountains themselves. And soon after that she found out where they were staying the night. It was no expensive hotel, not even a cheap one, not even a guest-house—but, unbelievably, a caravan. A tiny caravan tucked into the corner of a field on a headland overlooking the sea. Caron could hardly believe it. 'We're staying *here*?'

'That's right.' There was a gleam in his eyes as he spoke.

'But that's impossible.' Her voice was sharp with disapproval and she glared at him fiercely. 'It's quite out of the question.'

'Why?' he asked smoothly.

'Because—well, because it's not—ethical.'

His thick eyebrows rose. 'Ethical? You think I might pressurise you into doing something you don't want to do?'

'Not at all,' she denied. 'You couldn't do that, I wouldn't let you.' Except that he already had! 'It's just that I expected a hotel—with separate rooms. If I'd known I'd——'

'Never have come,' he finished for her. 'Do you think I didn't know? Personally I think it's the perfect retreat. It belongs to an old college friend of mine and he's willing to let me use it for as long as I like.'

Caron gasped.

'But have no fear,' he assured her before she could object, 'we shall stay for no more than one night. It would be unfair to neglect John's business any longer. As things stand everyone's been briefed and there should be no problems.'

They got out of the car and Lawson unlocked the caravan. Caron followed him cautiously inside, discovering that it was clean and looked surprisingly comfortable despite being so small. Lawson heaved a box out of his boot which contained everything they would need: milk, eggs, bread, meat, vegetables. He had definitely come well prepared!

Caron did not even bother to unpack the pretty dress she had put into her overnight-case when under the impression that they would be staying in a hotel. There was no point in dressing up now; she would keep on the cotton skirt and blouse she had worn for travelling.

Once everything was put away Lawson suggested a walk down to the shore. A zig-zagged path led down the cliff and the sea was a wonderful azure-blue, surprisingly blue for this latitude, thought Caron, and the beach was golden and deserted. White breakers crashed over the coarse sand, gulls wheeled overhead, shags haunted the rugged cliffs, which provided a perfect backdrop for the bay.

The sombre mood which had cloaked Lawson earlier had gone and Caron felt her awareness of him sharpening. They searched for crabs in tiny rock-pools left by the ebbing tide and his nearness engulfed her. She wandered away, pretending to look for driftwood which she could use in flower arrangements, but he followed. There was no escaping him.

He did not actually touch her but the awareness she felt was, if anything, worse than if he had taken her into his arms and thoroughly kissed her. Every nerve-end became sensitised and if he kept it up she did not know how she was going to get through the weekend without giving herself away. It was probably all part of his plan. Lawson seemed to know instinctively how to arouse her.

By tomorrow, or tonight even, he knew she would be ready to melt into his arms.

Lawson insisted on cooking their supper himself, while Caron sat at the other end of the caravan with a magazine and kept out of his way. It was impossible to read, however; he was far too disturbing. She was aware of every movement he made, even the air became difficult to breathe. She wished things were different between them, she wished he wasn't married, she wished that he loved her!

The meal, spare ribs with sweetcorn and oven-roasted potatoes, was tasty and tender. Caron had thought that, sitting opposite Lawson at the tiny pull-up table, she would be unable to eat, but instead surprised herself by cleaning her plate.

For a long time afterwards they remained at the table, talking about careful topics like their favourite films and books, their likes and dislikes where food and drink were concerned, but Lawson was nevertheless still subtly invading her senses, and when he touched her fingers across the table Caron wanted to snatch them away—in fact she knew it would be the safest thing to do.

Instead she let him carry on, his thumb stroking and arousing, hooded eyes intent on her face, watching her mouth and tongue as she spoke, looking deeply into her own green eyes, disturbing, hypnotising. It was a form of seduction, she knew, and yet she hadn't the will-power to stop him.

Lawson himself put an end to it. 'I think we ought to wash up.'

It was so prosaic and so unexpected that she almost laughed, but there was a hoarseness to his voice which she was beginning to associate with desire. Therefore it was an excellent suggestion.

'As you cooked the meal, I'll do it,' she said lightly. 'Go down to the beach again, I'll join you later.'

Surprisingly he agreed, though his softly confident smile told Caron that he knew exactly the effect he'd had on her.

Caron took her time over the washing-up. She had no intention of joining Lawson. The weekend was turning into a highly explosive situation, although she had known the danger of that before setting out. In one respect, because she loved him, she was deliriously happy, in another she was desperately worried because he was after all a married man. At the same time she was fast discovering that there was nothing more painful than unrequited love.

It was almost dark when he returned. 'What happened to you?' he asked, though his knowledgeable smile told her that he knew why she had stayed away.

'I felt tired,' she lied, her heart thudding all over again. There was no space to avoid him. With every breath she drew she took part of him in. How she was going to get through the whole night without giving herself away, she did not know.

'In that case, I think it's time for bed.'

Caron hoped he wasn't planning to share the same bed. No matter how strongly she was attracted to him, no matter how deep this love she felt for him went, sleeping together was out of the question.

To her relief the seats pulled out to make two separate beds, one at either end of the caravan. After Lawson had set them up he went outside again to take a last breath of fresh air. Caron took the opportunity to undress and wash faster than she had ever done in her life, and shoot into the bed furthest away from the door.

When he finally climbed the steps her heart began to pound so hard that it hurt, and she listened with bated breath to the sounds of him undressing, the rustle of his shirt, his shoes being taken off one by one, the rasp of the zip on his jeans.

Even though her eyes were tightly closed she could picture him in his various stages of undress until in her mind's eye she saw him standing naked, a fine figure of a man, his body firm and hard, a man who took good care of himself.

The tap ran next and she heard him brushing his teeth and washing his face and she waited, hoping to hear the creak of the other bed. Instead she heard the soft pad of his footsteps coming towards her and suddenly knew that her fears were not unfounded. She felt herself go rigid. She wanted him, she wanted him desperately, but what she wanted did not count. She made herself remember Karl and the way he had used her—and that was what this man was going to do now. Use her! *Use her!*

She could pretend to be asleep but he wouldn't accept that, she knew, and she was still debating what to do when he said mildly, 'I hate to disturb you, Caron, but my pyjamas are under that pillow.'

Her eyes shot open as relief rushed through her, but her voice was sharp. She had not seen him put anything under the pillow, and felt sure he was lying. 'You should have told me which bed to sleep in. Shall I go into the other one?' Wearing just a brief pair of underpants, he was still a threatening figure. His body was as hard and flat as she had imagined and her mouth went dry just looking at him.

'I wouldn't dream of disturbing you to that extent,' he growled. 'Just lift up so that I can get them.'

Obediently Caron raised herself on her elbows and let him slide his hand beneath the pillow. She could feel the warmth of him, smell the clean, minty freshness of his breath, and he seemed to be taking an awfully long time about it.

His pyjamas, when he finally retrieved them, consisted of nothing more than a pair of black boxer shorts. He could as easily have slept without them, she thought, convinced that they were an excuse.

So deep was the intensity of his gaze as he stood looking down at her that Caron felt the blood tingling through her veins, setting her whole body alive with throbbing urgency.

When he finally moved away it seemed like an effort on his part and Caron knew that his original plan had definitely been to climb into bed with her. Whatever the reason for changing his mind, she was glad. She did not want to have to fight him because she knew she would be fighting herself as well.

For long moments after she heard him settle her body felt on fire and she knew that sleep would be impossible. No matter how desperately she tried to steel herself against him, no matter how many times she told herself he was married and it was pointless loving him, no matter how many times she told herself she was a fool for thinking the way she did, she yearned for him so intensely that it hurt.

She lay awake for what seemed like hours, hearing the steady rhythm of the water, the cry of a sea-bird, Lawson's deepened breathing!

It infuriated her that he should sleep easily while she lay as wide awake as if it were the middle of the day. A hot drink might help but everything was at the other end of the caravan—near to Lawson's bed! Disturbing him could prove fatal. And yet the longer she lay there tossing and turning, the less likelihood there was of getting to sleep.

In the end, when she could stand it no longer, Caron got quietly out of bed and tiptoed across the floor. Beneath the thin quilt she could dimly make out Lawson's hunched shape and she stood looking down at him for a few spine-tingling seconds. Insanely she wanted to reach out and touch him, to stroke the thick blackness of his hair, feel the shape of his face and maybe press her lips against his skin. Her whole body pulsed with an emotion that shocked her by its intensity and it was all she could do to turn away.

It was a tighter squeeze to get at the sink and stove than she had imagined. Perhaps she ought not to bother with a hot drink, perhaps just a glass of milk? The tiny refrigerator was situated close to the head of his bed. She edged alongside and carefully opened the door, reaching out for the bottle and filling her glass. Still with the bottle in her hand, she took a sip. It was cool and delicious.

'You can pour one for me too.'

Lawson's voice startled her so much that the bottle slipped from her fingers, bounced on the edge of the sink and toppled over on to his bed.

'You clumsy idiot!' As the liquid began to seep through his quilt he sprang up and switched on the light.

'You shouldn't have frightened me,' Caron protested, picking up the bottle and searching for a cloth to mop up the milk, which was fast soaking more deeply into his bedclothes. 'I didn't know you were awake.'

'If you insist on wandering around in the middle of the night, what do you expect?'

'I couldn't sleep,' she defended, 'and I was thirsty. You can't blame me for waking you, I was very quiet. You must be a light sleeper, that's all I can say.'

'What do you suggest we do now since there isn't a spare quilt?' Lawson's tone was cynical and Caron's breathing felt constricted as his blue eyes flickered over her short cotton nightdress as though trying to picture her naked body beneath. She was very conscious of her vulnerability.

'You'd better have my bed,' she said, swallowing hard. 'I shan't sleep now so I'll just sit here and read or something.'

'Or something?' he queried. 'Do you realise it's only two o'clock?'

Caron had actually thought it much later. 'It doesn't matter; if you find me a blanket to pull around my shoulders I'll be all right,' she insisted.

'An excellent suggestion, but as there are no blankets an entirely impractical one. Go back to bed, Caron, and try not to disturb me again.' His tone was harsh and, hoisting the quilt off the bed, he took it outside to drape over a bush.

Caron felt it hardly fair that she should be the one to get a comfortable night's sleep, but she was not going to argue. She scuttled back to the other end of the caravan and was curled safely beneath the quilt before he returned.

Having been of the firm opinion that she wouldn't get to sleep at all, Caron was astonished when she opened her eyes to see the sun creating dappled patterns on the curtains, Lawson's bed neatly stowed away, and no evidence at all that he had slept there last night. In fact he was nowhere in sight.

She washed and dressed quickly and was making herself a cup of coffee when he appeared. 'So the girl who professes she can't sleep is finally up.'

Eager to get dressed before he returned, Caron had not looked at her watch; now she saw that it was almost ten and she turned wide, startled eyes on him. 'I had no idea. You should have woken me.'

'You looked too comfortable and too beautiful to be disturbed.'

It was a wry comment and her cheeks flushed at the thought of him watching her while she was asleep. 'I've never slept this late before, only once when I was ill. Have you eaten yet?'

He shook his head.

'Then I'll cook our breakfast; it's the least I can do.'

Across the tiny table as they ate their bacon and egg there was again no escaping him. Caron burned with a passion that astonished her. Even to look at Lawson filled her with sensation and longing, and hiding it from him was the hardest thing she had ever had to do.

She mopped up the remains of her egg with the last piece of bacon and lifted the fork to her mouth. Lawson watched her, his eyes narrowed on her lips as they parted to accept the food. His appraisal triggered off fresh sensations and as she moved her feet in unconscious response she encountered his beneath the table. Contact was devastating.

'You have a very sensual mouth, Caron.' His tone was soft and low. 'The sort of mouth men want to kiss. But you must know that—you're a very sensual person. Do you miss not having a man in your life?'

Caron had the feeling that something had prompted these words, but she did not know what and she looked at him warily. 'I don't crave a man for the sake of sex, if that's what you mean.'

His thick black brows rose. 'That's exactly what I mean.'

Her chin lifted. 'May I be permitted to ask what has prompted these thoughts?' She tucked her feet under the seat, as far away from his as possible, clamping her lips into a thin, tight line.

'Because I'm human and I thought maybe you were too. Sleeping here with you last night, seeing you in your nightdress, watching you as you slept have all had a profound effect on me.'

'Meaning,' said Caron, 'that you're hoping I feel the same and will be willing to—to let you use my body? Not only willing but in need of it as well?' Her green eyes flashed as she struggled up from the table. 'You're mistaken if you think I'll agree. You have no idea how I feel.'

'Oh, I think I do,' he drawled easily, sliding out too and standing as close as it was possible to get without their bodies actually touching. 'I know that at any time during this last twenty-four hours I could have taken you and you would have put up nothing more than a token resistance.'

Caron closed her eyes to blot out the cynical confidence on his face. 'You know nothing.'

'More than you think, my dear.' He pushed his face close up to hers, a confident smile curving his lips, his hands on her shoulders. 'And do you know what, Caron? I'm going to prove it.'

His mouth descended, crushing her lips, and Caron felt the caravan whirl even as she fought to free herself. It was a savage, intense kiss that seemed to be born of desperation. Was he using her as a substitute for

Stephanie? Was that what all this was about? Was he not seeing her at all but this other woman who was his wife?

Even though the feelings that raged inside her were like nothing she had ever experienced, Caron knew that she had to deny them. With a kind of desperate strength she pulled away from him and, swinging her arm in an arc, slapped him sharply across the face.

Her action caught him completely by surprise, gave him no time at all to defend himself, but to give him credit he did not even flinch. Caron saw his cheek go first white and then red, and for a second was appalled by her rashness, then her chin jutted and she said firmly, 'You're not using me as a substitute. If you need a woman that desperately then go back to your wife.'

The caravan became filled with tension, long, long seconds when neither of them spoke. Caron wondered whether she had gone too far and was preparing to apologise when he said, in a voice completely devoid of emotion, 'My wife is dead.'

Caron looked at him in stunned disbelief. 'Stephanie is dead?' she breathed. She could not believe it. When had it happened? How had he heard? Why hadn't he told her? It couldn't be true. It simply couldn't.

'Not Stephanie, no,' he said, shaking his head, 'she's my sister-in-law, she's nothing at all like Josie. Stephanie's a wonderful woman—but unfortunately there are not many like her around,' he added bitterly.

'And she came to tell you about—your wife?' Caron asked gently as the truth suddenly became clear. The black mood that had come upon him when Stephanie left, it made sense now.

He inclined his head in acknowledgement. 'Among other things, yes. Not that I'm emotionally hurt, you understand. Josie and I were divorced, there was no love lost between us. I'm genuinely sad, though, that it happened; it's not something I would wish on anyone, not even my worst enemy.'

'Was she ill?'

A snort of anger brought his head up with a jerk. 'Josie's sickness was other men. I wonder which poor bastard she was with when the accident happened? She was completely without morals, Caron.' Lawson's eyes narrowed on her as he spoke, bright blue and cold. 'The same as you! The same as my mother! Perfidious, all women. Except perhaps Stephanie.' His voice softened fractionally as he mentioned the other girl's name. 'But I'm finished, I have no intention of ever getting married again. I'll take my pleasure when and where I like but I'll never trust another woman.'

Caron had felt a brief flare of hope but it faded just as quickly upon hearing those harsh words. He might have fallen in love with Stephanie if she had not been married to his brother, but she herself stood no chance. And all because she had given him the wrong impression in the first place!

'I'm sorry, Lawson.' Caron touched his arm lightly. 'Did you—have you—any children?'

'No, thank goodness,' he breathed.

'Don't you like children?' she asked, detecting something in his tone.

'I think sometimes we're better off without them.'

Caron frowned. 'Why do you say that?'

'It doesn't matter,' he growled, pacing up and down the caravan. 'Life never goes the way we want, surely you've found that out? I plan to make myself beholden to no one. I'll live my life as I want, alone, and to hell with everyone else.'

He was not making a lot of sense but Caron knew better than to ask any further questions. She turned away and began to clear the table and when he suggested they go home she shrugged her shoulders and agreed. What was the point in staying and perhaps increasing the tension?

It was a silent, tortuous journey, far worse than on the way down, and Caron was relieved when they got back to the stables and both went their separate ways.

John, when she visited him that evening, was as astonished to hear about Lawson's wife as she had been. 'Why did he let you think Stephanie was his wife?'

Caron lifted her shoulders. 'Don't ask me; I fail to understand the man.'

'And you, how do you feel? I know you care about him even though you're always trying to deny it.'

'Lawson has no intention of ever re-marrying,' she told him firmly. 'He's made that quite clear. I shall be relieved when you're well enough to take over and he can go back to wherever it is he comes from.'

'As a matter of fact I have some good news,' her brother admitted triumphantly. 'I'm being let out of here tomorrow. I'll still be on crutches of course, but at least I'll be home. And Liz has promised to come and visit me. Isn't that wonderful?'

'Then you won't need Lawson any more?' The thought made Caron surprisingly sad, and it didn't occur to her that only a second ago she had declared that she wanted him to leave.

'I don't think I'll be quite ready to take over.' John grimaced. 'I shall need him for a while longer. And you never know, he might change his mind about marriage.'

Caron doubted it. Lawson had been very positive in his statement. He would use her body if she let him, but there would be no emotions involved, none at all. Josie had turned him into a very cynical, bitter and suspicious man.

Overnight she made up her mind that there could be nothing between them ever again. Always there had been some faint hope that one day... But now she knew that the chances of a serious relationship developing were nil and if he wanted anything from her it was to satisfy a basic male urge and nothing more.

The first thing she said to him the next morning when he came into the office to check the bookings was that John was coming home.

She was unprepared for his reaction. He looked totally stunned. 'He's well enough to take over again?'

'Not yet,' she assured him.

'But it won't be long before he is? My time here is almost at an end?' He looked saddened by the thought. 'Will you miss me when I go?'

Caron did not know how to answer this unexpected question; it would be so easy to give herself away. 'I'd be lying if I said I wouldn't miss you, but only as I would a sore thumb,' she lied bravely.

A quick, angry frown scored his brow. This was obviously not the answer he had expected and she waited for his harshly derogatory words, but instead he abruptly changed the subject. 'I think John will be pleased at the progress we've made. Takings are up on last year and bookings have never been so good.' With that he walked out of the office.

Caron regretted having said those untrue words but it had been an instinctive defence and in all probability was the best thing she could have done. She was totally devastated by the news that Lawson did not want to get married again and felt like crawling into a hole somewhere and crying her eyes out. But no way would she ever let him know that. At all costs she must protect herself.

John came home by ambulance just before lunch, surprisingly adept on his crutches, beaming all over his face, and in the days that followed Caron found that he was quite capable of running the office. If anyone was *de trop* it was herself.

Lawson frequently conferred with her brother and when John asked him to join them for an evening meal Caron knew exactly what lay behind the invitation. She tried to get out of it, she tried saying that it would be too much for him, that she had other things to do, but John would not listen. 'It's the least we can do. Lawson's proved himself an invaluable friend.'

Liz was invited too, which would help, thought Caron, except that she had no wish to be paired off with Lawson. She had done her best to avoid him this last couple of days, and it had been comparatively easy, but tonight there would be no getting away from him.

CHAPTER FIVE

CARON finished early to prepare the meal—not that she was going to a great deal of trouble; egg mayonnaise for starters, lemon chicken, and a chocolate fudge pudding, which was John's favourite. She wore a simple Indian cotton sundress in jewel shades of blue and green, the minimum of make-up, and drop earrings in an iridescent kingfisher-blue.

Despite the fact that she did not want Lawson spending the evening with them Caron could not stop the clamour of her heart as eight o'clock drew near. Liz had already arrived, looking fresh and lovely in a lemon chiffon blouse and matching linen skirt, and she and John could hardly take their eyes off each other.

It was the first time John had seen his new girlfriend in anything other than her nurse's uniform and he was completely taken aback. Caron guessed that she and Lawson wouldn't even be noticed. There had actually been no need to invite him; she could have cooked their meal and then made herself scarce instead of having to pretend that she was enjoying herself.

The doorbell rang and her hands twisted nervously as she went to let Lawson in. He wore a pair of blue lightweight trousers which matched the colour of his eyes, an even lighter blue shirt, and grey leather shoes that she imagined had cost the earth. He looked immaculate and devastatingly handsome and every one of her senses leapt in response.

She stepped back, said, 'Do come in,' and was surprised at how breathless she sounded.

His smile was cynical and he hesitated as he drew abreast, his hand lifting to touch her cheek. 'Why does something tell me that you're not looking forward to this evening?'

Caron widened her eyes. 'Nothing could be further from the truth.'

'You're forgetting, my friend,' he said with a confident smile, 'that I know you better than you know yourself. You're as nervous as a kitten.'

And it was all his fault! One glance out of those sensual blue eyes turned her whole world upside-down—and he knew it! Even now he was in no hurry to move his hand, his thumb stroking the soft skin behind her ear, his eyes locked into hers, causing her pulses to race in response.

It was the old game all over again. He was after her body but nothing more. She wriggled free. 'Please, I must go and see to the dinner. John and Liz are through there, I'll be with you in a few minutes.'

In the kitchen she took several steadying breaths before checking the vegetables. No matter how she tried, she could not find the strength to resist Lawson's advances. She ought to tell him firmly that she wanted nothing to do with him, she ought to rebuff every single attempt he made to touch her, but somehow she couldn't. She loved him and wanted him and needed him and there was no way she could deny those feelings.

When she entered the sitting-room Lawson's intense blue eyes were the first thing she saw, watching her progress across the room, sardonic amusement twisting his mouth, as though he knew exactly what thoughts were going through her mind. She encountered his gaze for a few seconds, no more, keeping her expression deliberately cool, before looking across at her brother and Liz.

The girl was sitting on the arm of John's chair, her hands were in his, and the love that shone from her eyes was there for them both to see. Envy, that they could be so free with their feelings, tore through Caron's throat. She took a swift, painful breath and turned away.

At her side Lawson muttered, 'I hope John knows what he's doing.'

'Trust you to think that there's no chance of their finding happiness,' she riposted fiercely. 'I happen to think that Liz is perfect for him.'

'Who knows what a person's like until you've lived with them?' he grunted.

'So you've been through a bad time,' she retorted. 'It doesn't mean every girl's the same.'

'No?' He looked at her with scorn. 'In my books they are.'

John's voice interrupted them. 'Hey, you two, when are we going to eat? Liz and I are starving.'

'It's ready when you are,' Caron smiled, willingly turning away from Lawson. 'Come and take your seats.'

The whole evening was a failure as far as Caron was concerned. Sometimes the conversation involved the four of them but more often than not John and his nurse were so intent on each other that it was up to her to entertain Lawson. And how did you entertain a man who had confessed that he would never trust women again, but simply take his pleasure from them? Whom you loved to distraction but knew you had to fight? It was an impossible, no-win situation.

After their meal she went into the kitchen to wash up, thinking she might get away from Lawson for a few minutes. It was a foolish hope; he followed and insisted on helping. 'It's really not necessary,' she protested when he picked up a towel. 'You're a guest. Why don't you go back and join the others?'

'Because, as you very well know, they're in a world of their own. They don't want me intruding.'

'Nor do I need you here,' she told him coldly.

'I think you're mistaken, I think you need me very much,' he growled.

Caron flashed him a look of scorn and turned towards the sink, running the taps and squeezing washing-up liquid into the bowl. She was unprepared when his hands slid around her waist and pulled her hard against him. She closed her eyes and tried to shut him out of her mind but it was impossible when he was so close, when she could feel his hard-muscled strength against her, when she could breathe him in, when every one of her senses stirred in response. Trying to deny herself of this man was like trying to deny life itself.

'Please.' Her plea came out as a breathless whisper. 'Please, Lawson, leave me alone.'

'You don't mean that.' He twisted her to face him and his hands cupped her face so that she was compelled to look into his eyes, which had darkened with desire, and she knew that her own eyes must be showing her need in a similar manner. Though she could use words to deny what she felt, there were so many other little things that gave her away. Her whole body at this moment was charged with emotion and there was not a thing she could do about it.

His lips came down on hers with devastating swiftness and although sanity told her to fight her response was automatic. She could not stop herself from returning his kiss. The taste of his lips was like a drug. She wanted him forever and ever. She wanted more of him than just this, she wanted him to love her as she loved him. Oh, God, why, why had she fallen in love with a man who had no intention at all of getting married again?

The kiss lasted no more than a few seconds and when Lawson let her go he grinned triumphantly. 'Point proven, don't you think?'

'You're a swine,' she spat.

'Let's wash up,' he said.

For the rest of the evening Caron felt as though her body did not belong to her. It was utterly and totally responsive to Lawson, tingling with feeling, almost melting with need, and he made sure that she stayed that way. Not by words or deeds, simply by looking at her, his narrowed eyes searching out each sensitive area, lingering, doing heaven knew what to her in his thoughts.

When Liz finally, reluctantly said she must go or she would never be up for work the next morning, Lawson, to Caron's intense relief, rose to leave too. He shook John's hand. 'It's been a most enjoyable evening.'

John nodded. 'We must do it again some time.'

Caron followed Lawson to the door, leaving her brother and Liz to say their goodnights alone. She wanted Lawson to kiss her again, expected it even, and she could not believe it when, with nothing more than a knowing grin, he walked away. 'I'll see you in the morning,' he said.

She felt like picking up the nearest object and hurling it after him. He knew exactly how she felt. It had been a deliberate attempt on his part to prove that she was fooling no one, not even herself. But what he did not know was how strongly she felt about letting any man make love to her. It would never happen again out of wedlock, never! She might love Lawson with every fibre of her being, but it made no difference.

The highlight of Caron's day was normally her early morning ride. They were times when she felt as free as the wind through her hair, at one with the galloping beast, times when she could forget Lawson, forget all her problems, and enjoy only the feeling of freedom.

But the next morning she was allowed no such pleasure. Lawson was in the paddock before her, swinging himself up on to Hunter with what looked like an effort. 'I thought I'd join you.'

'And if I say I don't want you to?' asked Caron, her green eyes flashing very real anger as she lifted the saddle over her horse and tightened the girth with ease born of practice. These moments were precious and she did not want anyone, especially Lawson, spoiling them.

'It will make no difference,' he told her, trying without much success to steady the prancing horse.

'I really would prefer to ride alone,' she told him distantly. 'You're invading my privacy. This is a time of day I always keep for myself.' The harness was in place, the bit in the horse's mouth, and she expertly mounted, feeling better now that she was on Lawson's level. There was something unnerving about him towering so high above her.

'Yes, I've seen you,' he admitted. 'I've watched you ride often.' His blue eyes were steady on hers but she had no way of knowing what he was thinking.

It did not please her to discover that he had been watching her when she was unaware of it, and her lips clamped that little bit tighter. She had not yet forgiven him for what he had done to her last night. Emotions had raged through her body for many hours before she finally fell asleep, and even now, in the midst of her anger, she still felt the pull of his magnetism.

'You're good, very good,' he added.

'That wasn't your opinion when we first met,' she told him coldly, her chin high.

He shrugged his broad shoulders indifferently. 'Maybe I was wrong. Let's go, you can lead the way.'

Caron could see that she was not going to win. 'OK, we'll ride together, just this once,' she added reluctantly. 'But remember in future that I prefer to ride alone.'

Out of the paddock, for the first half-mile, they trotted silently side by side. Caron, stealing a glance at Lawson, saw that he was smiling to himself, as though enjoying some private joke. This was all part and parcel of some game, she thought furiously, and the next moment she found out what it was.

'Let's have a race,' he said, blue eyes challenging. 'If I win you come out to dinner with me at the Shamrock tonight.'

Never one to turn down a bet, Caron nodded. She had quickly summed up the situation. Lawson was a complete novice when it came to riding; he wasn't even sitting correctly. When he borrowed Hunter it must have been to teach himself to ride, too embarrassed to ask for proper lessons. Maybe with this plan in mind?

'You're on,' she said with a huge grin. It would probably be the first time in his life that he had ever been humiliated by a woman.

'We'll go to that oak tree out there——' he pointed into the distance '—and back to the stable.'

'Right.' Even as she spoke Caron urged her horse forward, adrenalin already high. This was going to be a walk-over. Her hair streamed out behind like spun gold and there was grim determination on her face. All that could be heard was the thunder of drumming hoofs and when she risked a glance over her shoulder she saw that Lawson was several yards behind.

He did not look daunted by it. In fact he risked letting go the horse's rein with one hand to give her a mocking salute. The nerve of the man, she thought.

When they reached the tree and turned he had made up a couple of yards. Not unduly worried, Caron spurred her horse on to even greater effort, but when Lawson drew level halfway on the home run she knew she was in trouble unless she managed to hold him off.

It was neck and neck all the way after that, until ten yards from the stables Hunter, apparently without any further urging on Lawson's part, galloped home an easy winner. Caron could not believe it and she was furious with herself for letting him beat her. Lawson was certainly no novice. He had tricked her; he had known all along that he stood an excellent chance of winning. He had actually deliberately held back until the very end. She could murder him.

'You knew you were going to win, didn't you?' she demanded crossly.

His smile was all triumphant. 'I never bet on anything I'm not certain of.'

'You let me think you weren't a very good rider,' she accused.

'Because I knew you wouldn't take me on otherwise.' His blue eyes locked into hers. 'Isn't that so?'

'You're dead right,' she spat, trying to ignore the surge of emotion that coursed through her. 'Why do you want to take me out anyway? To try and force me into your bed at the end of the evening? Is that the plan? Are you going to ply me with drink again and hope you'll be in luck?'

'I heard John invite Liz. I thought it would give them an opportunity to have some time to themselves,' he answered carelessly.

'In that case I can easily amuse myself,' she retorted crossly. 'I don't have to go anywhere with you.' She slid down and began taking off the harness and saddle.

'At the expense of turning myself into a bore, might I again say how very beautiful you are when you're angry?'

He was so close behind her that their bodies were almost touching, and Caron's heart beat painfully fast, but her tongue was still sharp as she spoke. 'Sweet words will get you nowhere.'

'The most beautiful woman I've ever met.'

'You're wasting your time.' She refused to turn and look into eyes which she knew could range from deepest cobalt to palest ice-blue, eyes which could melt her at a glance or whip her raw.

'Dress up for me tonight, my beautiful friend; I think we might make it an evening to remember.'

Caron felt a river of fire shoot from her throat to her groin. He was suddenly relentless in his pursuit of her and wanting him and needing him as she did it was going to be achingly difficult to hold him at bay. 'I've not yet said that I'll come,' she told him sharply.

'But you lost the bet,' he insisted, 'and I'm sure you're not the type of girl to back out.'

Caron finally turned to face him, meeting eyes that were mockingly amused. 'You're right, I'm not—of course I'll come out with you—for a meal. As for anything else, forget it.'

His brows rose. 'Your only battle is with yourself, my dear.' And with a complete change of subject, 'If you want to get back to cook John's breakfast I'll see to the horses.'

Caron could not get away from him quickly enough and for the rest of the day she tried to think up an excuse not to go out with him. But when her brother hinted that Liz was coming again she knew she had no choice in the matter.

She dressed with care for her evening out. Not because Lawson had insisted but because she needed it as armour against him. She needed to feel beautiful and confident and able to combat anything he might throw at her.

Pink was a colour that suited her best and her simple silky dress with its opera top and slightly flared skirt was neither too sophisticated nor too plain.

Lawson was prompt as usual, but Caron's heart had begun thudding long before he put in an appearance. It was insanity loving a man who had sworn never to get married again, but what could she do about it? She could only pray that one day he would change his mind. Perhaps she would be the one to do it for him? What a hope that was. He was as stubborn as a mule and would probably spend the rest of his life breaking a few hearts but ending up a lonely old man.

He wore the same blue trousers as yesterday with a white shirt through which she could see the black hairs that roughened his chest. Just looking at him excited her and when he took her hands and pressed a kiss to her brow the earth moved beneath her feet. She would enjoy the next few hours, she determined in that moment; she would forget that he wasn't serious about her, that none of this meant a thing. She would take what he was offering and pop it into her bag of memories for the cold years that lay ahead.

The whole evening took on a magical air. He was far more attentive than he had ever been before and he had to be blind not to see the love shining out of her eyes. Caron desperately craved physical contact and it was with the greatest difficulty that she stopped herself from reaching out and touching him.

After their meal he drove to the edge of a lough where the mountains beyond were lost in a soft mist and the whole area took on an unreal texture. They stood and looked at the silent water for several long minutes, shoulders touching, minds attuned, before he gently turned her to face him. Looking deep and long into the luminous beauty of her eyes, he took her into his arms and moulded her unresisting body against his.

As his lips came down on hers Caron's arms went involuntarily around him. This was what she had been hungering for all evening, what had been gnawing away inside, and her whole body became a mass of sensation. It went fleetingly through her mind that she ought to resist him, and she made a token effort of trying to push him away, but he stopped her with a fierce, 'Oh, no, Caron, not this time.'

Time began to lose all meaning. His kiss assaulted her senses, she gloried in the feel and taste of his mouth, of the hardness of his body, of the need and desire that ran like mercury through every one of her veins, culminating its intensity in her groin.

All sensible thoughts deserted her as she opened her mouth freely, whimpering her pleasure at the mutual exploration, both of them feeling a desperate hunger born of keeping their distance for too long.

Caron's heart beat frantically within her chest as though trying to get out. She felt on fire, her legs trembling so much that if Lawson let her go she would collapse. She clung to him for dear life, aware of a similar urgency pounding through his own heated body.

When they drew apart for breath she voiced a faint, choking protest. 'Lawson, no, this is——'

'This is what you've wanted all along,' he finished savagely for her. 'Don't try to deny it.'

He was right, and when he claimed her mouth yet again she lost all thoughts of objecting. This time he seduced her senses, running the tip of his tongue tantalisingly over her lips, feathering her face with kisses before searing a trail down her throat. He seemed to know instinctively her most sensitive areas.

He slipped down one of her dress-straps, revealing and cupping the soft fullness of her breast. His fingers teased her nipple until it hardened to his touch and Caron arched into him, feeling as though she were going to faint with sheer pleasure.

There was no thought now of rejecting him. She felt nothing but the heady sensation of unexpected arousal, a primitive passion that she had never felt before and never expected to feel again. 'Lawson,' she breathed, overcome with a burning need that only he could assuage.

'My beautiful Caron.' His mouth took the place of his hand and Caron's head fell back as she savoured the tortuous pleasure. Her stomach tightened and quivered as first his tongue and then his teeth grazed and nipped and drew out of her a response she had never dreamt of, never felt before.

Mindless with desire, she ground her hips against his and felt the full strength of his arousal. Whimpering incoherently, she buried her face in his hair. His hands moved over her hips and thighs, feeling the heat of her skin through the thin silk of her dress.

'Caron, I want you—but not here,' he added roughly, and with his arm about her waist, her shoulder tucked into him, her acquiescence taken for granted, he walked her to his car, thighs brushing, hearts pounding, nothing else mattering at this moment except this aching need for each other.

Lawson started the engine and they headed back towards the cottage. Constantly he glanced at her, touching her, squeezing her hand, making sure that none of her feelings were allowed to fade. Caron knew that if she let him make love to her it would be the biggest mistake of her life, but for once all sane reasoning had fled.

At first they did not notice the orange glow in the sky; they were far too intent on each other, far too anxious to get home and assuage these desires that were so fierce they almost hurt.

But as they drew closer they could not miss the strange light. 'It looks as though there's a fire somewhere,' said Lawson with a frown, and unconsciously put his foot down on the accelerator.

As they topped a hill they could see tongues of angry flame leaping into the sky and it suddenly became frighteningly obvious that the fire was in the vicinity of the riding stables.

Caron's hands came to her mouth and her heart stopped beating. 'Oh, no! *Oh, no!* Please, don't let it be our house, please don't let John be hurt again.'

It grieved her to think that she had been enjoying Lawson's lovemaking while her brother's life was in danger. John was in no condition to escape swiftly if the fire caught him unawares. What if he were trapped indoors? What if...?

The car was fairly flying along the road now, Lawson's face taut with concentration. 'There's no telling yet exactly where the fire is,' he told her grimly, but it was plain by his anxious expression that he was of the same mind as she.

Not until they were within half a mile did it become clear that it wasn't the riding stables but the forest near by. Timber crackled and smoke belched and everywhere was the acrid smell of burning wood.

Caron could not describe her relief; it washed over her in wave after wave of raw emotion that left her shaky and faintly nauseous. Then she saw that the fire was slowly moving towards the house and her fear for John's safety renewed itself.

'We must make sure John's not inside,' she yelled, scrambling out of the car when he stopped because a police car blocked the road. She began running, only to find her arm caught by a burly policeman.

'I'm afraid you can't go any nearer, miss.'

'But I live there,' she protested fiercely. 'And my brother's inside the house. I must get him out; he's got a broken leg and——'

'Everyone's been evacuated, miss, there's no need to panic.'

'Where is he, then? Where is my brother?' she shrieked, close to hysteria now. 'And how about the horses? Has anyone thought about moving them?' She heard a faint neigh of fear and with a cry she wrenched herself free and went running along the road.

Lawson caught her up. 'Caron, don't do anything foolish.'

'But it's John's livelihood that's at stake,' she insisted. 'We must move the horses.'

As they drew closer, however, she could see that the horses were in no danger, that the fire was sweeping away in the opposite direction. 'What if the wind changes, though?' she asked Lawson anxiously.

'Caron, you're worrying for nothing.' He put his arm comfortingly about her shoulders. 'The firemen have it all under control.'

They stood and watched as the hoses jetted fierce arcs of water both into the flames and the area around the fire so that it could spread no more.

But Caron was still anxious about John and, pulling away from Lawson, she ran across to the chief fire officer, who was standing a few yards away. In reply to her anxious questions he informed her that her brother had been taken to a house in the village. 'Purely as a precaution,' he added. 'But the fire's already under control, you have no need to worry about the house. Unlike the poor man who lives in that cottage in the woods. We haven't been able to trace him yet, but——'

'But what?' barked Lawson, who had followed and heard every word. 'That's my cottage, what's happened?'

The fireman grimaced compassionately. 'It's gutted, sir. We can't be sure yet but we think that's where the fire started.'

Caron felt Lawson go tense at her side and she looked up at him with horror on her face. 'Oh, Lawson, it can't be true.'

'I'm afraid it is, miss,' confirmed the officer, 'and we'll need to talk to you tomorrow, sir.'

Lawson nodded. 'Of course. I'll do anything I can to help you with your enquiries.'

As the officer walked away to have words with one of his men Caron clung to Lawson's arm. 'I can't believe it. Your cottage—everything—gone. It's so awful. How could it have happened? Do you think someone set fire to it deliberately?'

'Arson?' he asked with a quick frown. 'I shouldn't think so. I have no enemies who would want to destroy me.'

'Then what could have caused it?'

He shook his head. 'I really have no idea.'

'It's so awful. You've lost everything.' And she hadn't given his cottage a thought, she had been conscious only of her brother.

'A few clothes, that's all,' he derided. 'There was nothing of value in the cottage. Perhaps it's an omen. Time I went home.'

'John's still depending on you.' Her throat felt dry and tight and her voice sounded husky and unnatural. She hoped he would put it down to the shock and the smoke that filled the air, and not guess at her very real anguish.

'Naturally I won't let him down, but as soon as he can cope I shall go. Come, let's find John and reassure him that his home and business are safe.' There was nothing now in his tone to suggest that he desired her. It had gone, all in a matter of minutes. Not for him the agony of love that burned and threatened to destroy. There would be another occasion, another time when he wanted to make love to her, when he desired her body, but during the hours and probably days in between she would play little part in his thoughts. Caron felt suddenly bitter and swore to herself that she would never, ever let him get through to her again. She would hide her love completely, never let it see the light of day.

John was with Mary O'Donnell, the village shop-keeper, and he looked up in concern as the woman showed them into her comfortable sitting-room, getting up from his seat, still leaning heavily on his crutch, making Caron realise how difficult it would have been for him to get out speedily if the need had arisen.

'How bad is it?' he wanted to know.

Lawson answered him quickly and reassuringly.

'Have you heard how it started?'

'If I'm to believe the fire officer, in my cottage,' confirmed Lawson with a grimace, 'though I can't think how.'

Disbelief widened John's eyes. 'Does that mean it's—burnt out completely?' And when Lawson nodded, 'Lord, man, that's awful. You must move in with us.'

Move in with them? It was the logical solution, the only one, and yet Caron was appalled by it. For however long Lawson remained she would be at his mercy, there would be no escape. Living with him, being close to him at all times, how could she hope to hide her feelings?

CHAPTER SIX

IN THE days and weeks that followed, Caron discovered that her fears were unfounded. Lawson was a perfect gentleman. Liz came around frequently and out of politeness Caron and Lawson kept out of their way, often going for long walks or meals out.

His cottage had been totally destroyed but fortunately the only personal possessions that he had lost were his clothes. After exhaustive tests it was decided that the fire had started with a spark from the fire, which he had thought was well and truly out.

He seemed in no hurry now to get her into his bed, taking his pleasure instead out of watching her reaction to him, and this was something she could not hide. On several occasions he lowered his voice to a sensual growl, observing with satisfaction the delicate colour rise under her skin. It was a game he never ceased to tire of playing.

One evening Liz managed to persuade John to let her take him for a drive. He was nervous now of going on the road, but when Liz assured him that she had been driving for years and had a very good track record he reluctantly agreed.

'It's the best thing for him,' said Lawson when they had gone. 'He's stayed in for far too long.'

John hadn't imprisoned himself solely in the house. With the aid of his crutches he had managed to get about the yard, though the uneven ground hadn't helped and on one occasion when he had fallen Caron had been sick with fear that he might have done further injury to himself. In fact all that had been hurt was his pride.

Now she and Lawson were alone in the house, completely alone for the first time. 'Perhaps we should go out too?' Caron suggested brightly. Even that would be better than staying in waiting for him to strike. She was sure it was only a matter of time before he attempted to make love to her again.

'I don't think so.' His smile was wide but held no humour. 'I realise, Caron, that you're not happy with the situation, but it's a bit silly when we both feel so strongly about each other, don't you think?'

'No! Never!' she exclaimed loudly. 'I lost my head on the night of the fire but it won't happen again, I assure you. I refuse to be used.'

He frowned harshly. 'You think that's what I'm planning to do, use you?'

'Of course. Didn't you say you would take your pleasure where and when you could find it?'

'Maybe I did in the heat of the moment, but——'

'In the heat of the moment?' scorned Caron. 'Come off it, Lawson, you're using me. Why don't you admit it?'

She was unprepared for the tautness of his jaw, the jerking muscles, the sudden hostility in his eyes. 'You think my mind's warped because of Josie's infidelity?' he barked fiercely.

'You've admitted it yourself.'

He gave a snort of anger. 'Perhaps it's time I told you the whole story. Perhaps then you might begin to understand how I feel.'

Caron frowned. 'What more is there to tell?'

He walked away from the window and sat down in one of the chairs. He suddenly seemed to have gone a long way away from her. Slowly she followed and sat down also, her green eyes intent on his face.

'We had a sister, Bruce and I. Did you know that?'

Caron shook her head, her eyes wide and startled. 'You've never mentioned her before.'

'With just cause,' he bit out grimly. 'She was an embarrassment.' And at her start of surprise, 'Not to me, never to me, I loved her dearly—but to my mother. That's what hurts most of all, my mother turning against her own daughter.'

Caron looked at him with eyes full of concern and curiosity.

'Oh, yes, my mother couldn't bear the thought that she had brought into the world a child who was physically disabled.' Lawson's hatred for his mother was clear by the disgust in his tone. 'She liked all things beautiful and everything had to be perfect. She was a beautiful woman herself.' A muscle jerked fiercely in his jaw. 'Once Emily was past the baby stage, but still in need of constant attention, my mother wanted her institutionalised.' He ignored Caron's gasp and went on, 'My father wouldn't hear of it, and it was up to the three of us to look after her.'

'Are you saying your mother didn't love her own daughter?' she asked in a shocked whisper.

He nodded, his mouth twisted and bitter. 'Over the years my mother went out more and more often. It got to the pitch when she was rarely at home. I didn't know at first that she was seeing other men; when I did find out I was disgusted.'

'Oh, Lawson.' Caron did not know what to say. It was hard to believe that any woman would feel so coldly detached towards her own flesh and blood.

'I don't want your pity,' he snarled. 'It's something that's over and done with.'

'So—what happened to your sister?' she asked, her tone husky with emotion.

'I'm coming to that,' he told her harshly. 'When Bruce grew up he could no longer stand the tension between our parents so he left home. Soon afterwards they were divorced and it was up to me and my father to look after Emily.'

He lapsed into silence for a few seconds. 'I've often wondered since whether we did the right thing in keeping her at home. My father gave up his job completely and I rarely went out myself in the evenings or at weekends. But the strain told on my father. I got home one day and——' his voice faltered '—my father was dead. His heart gave out under the pressure.'

Caron's hands went involuntarily over her mouth, her eyes wide and compassionate.

Lawson went on, 'When Bruce came home for the funeral he brought a girl with him. He said he was going to marry her. It was Stephanie. I'd never met anyone like her. She instantly made a fuss of Emily, doing her best to understand and help her. In fact,' he added sourly, 'she did everything my mother should have done.

'They stayed a few days and, seeing Stephanie with Emily, I wished I could meet someone like her, someone who would love my sister the way I did and who would help me look after her. There was no chance of Bruce moving back because he'd built his own life, he had his work and his friends, and it wouldn't have been fair even to suggest it.'

Having met Stephanie, Caron could appreciate what he was saying. She was a warm, loving and sincere person whom Lawson would probably have asked to marry him if he had met her first. And not solely because of Emily, but because he would not have been able to stop himself falling in love with her. Caron suspected that he was more than half in love with her anyway.

'Once I was on my own it was impossible for me to look after Emily without bringing in outside help, but I couldn't seem to find anyone who was prepared to give her the love that she needed. They looked after her physical needs, but that was all. I was at my wit's end because I was running my own printing company, which was doing far better than I'd ever anticipated, but it needed me if it was to continue being successful and I couldn't spare enough time for Emily. It seemed a hopeless situation until I met Josie.'

His lips twisted derisively as he spoke and Caron wanted to tell him that he need not go on, that he did not have to torture himself with unhappy memories. On the other hand she desperately wanted to hear the whole story.

'Josie seemed to be everything I was looking for. She had all of Stephanie's qualities, she loved me and was kind to my sister and above all I loved her. I wasn't such a cold-hearted bastard that I would marry a girl simply to provide my sister with a nurse. But as soon as we were married she changed.'

He paused as memories flooded in and it broke Caron's heart to see the hurt in his eyes.

'She didn't want to live in the family home, she said, she wanted another house, a new one, and she did not want Emily living with us. It caused a lot of arguments but because of my love for her I eventually gave in. Emily was put into a home. I can't tell you how it grieved me having to do that, and I went to see her every single day after I finished work, weekends as well.'

He drew in a ragged, tortured breath. 'It didn't help my marriage; I was accused of feeling more for Emily than I did for my wife and I heard a rumour that she was seeing other men. When I tackled her about it she said it was true but she promised to stop, saying that she loved me dearly, it was just that I wasn't spending enough time at home and she felt neglected.'

It was the old, old story, thought Caron, only in this instance it wasn't a consuming passion for his job that kept Lawson out late, but love for his sister. If only Josie could have shared that love then none of this would have happened.

'But she didn't change,' he went on, 'she still went out, still saw other men—*just like my mother*!' He spat the words savagely. 'We had a row of rows and I told her to pack her bags and go and not to come back. I filed for a divorce straight away. If only she had understood how I felt about my sister, it could have been so different. I did love Josie in the beginning, but she killed whatever affection I felt by her treatment of Emily. I was the only one who cared about Emily. Bruce went to see her, but not very often, and I couldn't just let her sit there and think that neither of us loved her any more.'

Caron's tears welled. There was compassion in this man that she had never dreamt existed.

'My sister died not long after our divorce.' He was still now, his eyes distant. 'Josie did not attend the funeral, she didn't even send her condolences. The rest you know. I came here after Emily died because I needed time to think, to put my mind at rest, to come to terms with all that had happened in my life.'

Caron knew that there was nothing she could say at this moment to ease his sorrow. 'I never knew you'd had so much hardship,' she murmured. 'Thank you for telling me.'

'I hope you've got the picture. I hope you realise now why I have no intention of ever falling in love again.' There was a bitter edge to his voice.

She nodded. It was truly an amazing story and she could see why he was so wary and mistrusting, but surely time would heal his wounds? 'All women aren't like Josie; you only have to look at Stephanie to see that,' she said softly.

'Too many of them are,' he snarled, 'and I'm not taking any more chances. And now we've got that out of the way let's get on with our evening. We were talking about giving free rein to our emotions, isn't that right?'

'*You* were talking about it,' she answered sharply. 'Personally I have no intention of having an affair with you. One day, no matter how you feel now, you'll find someone else to love, someone who won't let you down. And if you want a few flings in the meantime then that's your prerogative, but don't expect me to take part. The man who makes love to me will be the man I marry— it's as simple as that.'

'You sound as though you mean it.'

'I do,' she assured him, wondering what twist of fate had made her fall in love with a man who was so determined never to love again.

He slowly smiled. 'It would be interesting to see if I could persuade you to change your mind.'

Caron felt swift sensation run through her veins. It would be so easy for him. He only had to kiss her to start off a whole chain of emotions that were impossible to control. Even now simply looking at him, seeing his earthy sexuality made her want to rush into his arms.

It was with an effort that she controlled herself and forced deliberate hostility into her eyes. They flashed a vivid green as she looked at him, and the whole of her delicate body quivered with what looked like anger but was in fact suppressed desire.

'I knew John was making a mistake when he suggested you move in here,' she declared hotly. 'He has no idea how you've pestered me ever since we first met.'

'Oh, no,' said Lawson at once. 'You were the one who did the chasing, surely you remember that?'

'My interest in you had nothing to do with sex,' she told him coolly, 'and as far as I'm concerned it's never changed. So if all you're interested in tonight is my body then forget it. I'll cook us a meal, or we can go out. Or *you* can go out—that would be even better still. I'd really enjoy a night in by myself.'

His eyes gleamed with wry amusement. 'Do you know what I think? I think you're scared. I think you feel a whole lot more than you're admitting. Don't forget, over the last few weeks I've had every opportunity to observe you. You want me, Caron, as much as I want you. It's only your conscience that's stopping you.'

She shook her head. 'That's not true. I admit I'm as wary of men as you are of women, and, like you, I have no intention at this moment of getting married, although I'm not saying it can't happen in the future. But unlike you I don't need sexual fulfilment. I'm happy as I am. I enjoy working for my brother. Until I came here I didn't realise how much I missed the farm.'

'You're making excuses, Caron.' As he spoke Lawson got up and came towards her, his eyes intent on hers, causing the breath to catch in her throat. He halted directly in front of her, putting his hands on the arms of her chair and bending down until his face was a mere inch away from hers.

Caron's heart beat alarmingly loud and she touched the tip of her tongue to suddenly dry lips. It was a mistake. He took it as an invitation and the next second his mouth was moving with erotic slowness over hers.

At once every nerve-end became sensitised and it was all she could do to stop herself from hooking her arms around his neck and pulling him down. With a restraint she had not known she possessed Caron managed to keep still and pretend that his kiss meant nothing, even when his tongue traced a delicate path across her lips. Though the desire quivering to life inside her was torment indeed.

Lawson laughed softly, his warm, clean breath on her face. 'You don't fool me with that ice-maiden image, but the night is young, I'll wait for my pleasure.' He lifted himself away from her but instead of moving he stood for a few moments more, watching her, smiling softly, making sure she knew exactly how he felt and what she could expect before John and Liz returned.

'Meanwhile my stomach tells me that it's in need of sustenance. I think, Caron Lorimer, that I might cook us a meal myself. How does that sound?'

'It sounds pretty good.' Because it meant that she could keep out of his way. She could stay here and read or go up to her room, do anything in fact as long as she steered clear of the kitchen. An hour or so's respite was just what she needed.

'And you can keep me company. We'll sup wine while I work and you can entertain me with stories about the years you spent in London.'

Caron groaned inwardly and racked her brains for an excuse. 'I really must take a shower first and get changed.'

'Which will take you all of ten minutes, unless you intend to linger—in which case I shall be compelled to come looking for you.' His grin was wicked.

Caron knew Lawson well enough by now to realise that he meant what he said. 'I shan't be very long,' she assured him fiercely.

Although she was pleased for her brother she wished he had not gone out. John constantly said that she and Lawson made an ideal couple but had he any idea at all about the way she was being treated? Did he know that Lawson was interested in only one thing?

No, of course he didn't. She stood beneath the shower, still thinking about her brother. John seemed to have forgotten the fact that this dark-haired man had no intention of going through the whole painful affair of getting married ever again. Or was he trying to push them together because he no longer wanted her to make her home with him? Not now he had Liz. Was that it? Panic suddenly stampeded through Caron's veins and she swiftly towelled herself dry. She had come out here envisaging settling down and spending, if not the rest of her life, a good few years with her brother, and now, almost overnight, everything had changed.

She pulled on undies and a mint-green cotton dress, brushing her fine blonde hair until it shone like spun silk. She rarely used make-up—a dusting of eyeshadow and mascara and a touch of lipstick occasionally, that was all. She studied her reflection in the mirror, wondering whether to apply some now and was astonished to see that her eyes were bright and luminous, her cheeks flushed. And all because of that man downstairs!

In her absence Lawson had prepared vegetables and put lamb chops under the grill. The smells emanating from the kitchen were delicious, making Caron realise exactly how hungry she was. He looked up as she entered, his eyes roving approvingly over her slender body. 'I was just thinking about coming to fetch you.'

Caron looked at the clock on the wall. It had taken her ten and a half minutes precisely to get ready. 'I call it pretty good timing myself. Would you like me to lay the table?'

'Anything to get away from me?' he growled. He pushed a glass of wine into her hand and indicated one of the kitchen stools. 'Sit down and look beautiful. The table can wait. How long did you go out with this guy who turned you off men?'

Surprised by his abrupt question, Caron took a sip of the red liquid. Had he been thinking about Karl while she was upstairs? When he said he wanted to hear about the time she had spent in London, did he mean with the man she had been going to marry? 'I really don't see that it's any of your business,' she said curtly.

'As he hurt you so much I presume you must have been going out with him for a long time?'

Caron shrugged. 'Not really, about six months.'

'Did he ever make love to you?'

Her cheeks flooded with swift, guilty colour. 'But only because I thought I was going to marry him,' she defended quickly. 'I'm not the type of girl to go to bed with any man. And the next time I shall definitely be married, you can bet your bottom dollar on that.'

'I think if anyone was using you it was him,' he said quietly and thoughtfully.

'Personally I think all men are as bad as each other,' she snapped.

For a long, tension-filled second he looked at her and then, with a secret smile that made her wonder what he was thinking, changed the subject. 'I can't believe that you thought you'd be happy working as a secretary in a major city when you'd lived all your life on a farm. I'm amazed you stuck it as long as you did. How long did you say you were there?'

'Four years.'

'And now you're going to throw all your training and experience away and settle down here with your brother?'

'That was the general idea,' she admitted, 'but now John's met Liz I'm not so sure. They're talking about getting engaged. I doubt they'll want me around once they're married.'

'You could be right,' he agreed pleasantly. 'More wine?'

They were both silent for a few minutes after he had topped up her glass, both deep in their own thoughts. Caron wondered about his sister who'd had such a raw deal. It was difficult to imagine the Lawson she knew looking after her so lovingly and caringly. It was a side to his nature she had not yet been privy to, and probably never would.

Caron sipped her wine but it was not until she felt it going to her head that she knew she must be careful. It could be Lawson's intention to get her inebriated. He knew how easily she responded to him when she'd had a drink. She put the glass down and pushed it away from her, determined not to touch another drop, except with her meal.

She had not realised that Lawson was watching and had correctly guessed what was going through her mind. 'What is it that you're afraid of?' He was smiling though his voice held a touch of scorn. 'Getting drunk and losing your inhibitions? I can think of worse things.'

'I prefer to be in charge of my own body,' she tossed back smartly. 'I have no intention of waking up in the morning to find out that I've spent the night in your bed.'

'You think I'd deliberately get you drunk?'

She inclined her head. 'Yes, I do as a matter of fact.'

'Then you don't know me very well at all.' His eyes glittered with sudden anger. 'A drunken woman is not my idea of pleasure.'

Caron looked savagely back. 'This is a pointless conversation, I'm going up to my room. You can forget dinner, I don't want it.'

As she moved, his powerful hand gripped her wrist in a pulverising action that threatened to stem the flow of blood.

The way he sprang at her reminded Caron of that first day they had met when her horse was running away. He had sprung out of nowhere then, a giant of a man with invincible strength. And now he was using that strength on her again.

'Please,' she said icily, 'you're hurting.'

Immediately he released her but he did not move. 'We're eating together whether you like it or not.'

Caron lifted her narrow shoulders. 'OK, you win, I'll go and get the table ready.' She slipped out of the kitchen before he could say another word and although the isolation of her own room beckoned she resisted temptation. She laid the table with a crisp white cloth and matching napkins and if things had been different she would have put candles on it too. But this wasn't a soft lights and romantic music occasion. This was just her and the man whose only interest in her was physical.

The lamb chops were cooked to perfection and tasted delicious, the vegetables slightly crispy just as she liked them; even so she ate no more than a few mouthfuls, toying around with the food and eventually putting down her knife and fork.

'Is something wrong? You don't like it?' he asked fiercely, his blue eyes intent on hers.

'It's fine, I'm just not hungry,' she replied.

'There have been a lot of times lately when you haven't been hungry,' he growled. 'Is my presence in this house so abhorrent?' There was a grimness to his mouth as he spoke.

Caron decided that truth was better than a lie. 'How very discerning of you. That's exactly what's wrong with me. Ever since John invited you here I've been unhappy.'

His lips compressed, his eyes were a cold ice-blue which threatened to slice right through her. 'Then you might like to know that I'm leaving, that I'm going back to my home in Dublin in the very near future.'

Caron drew in a harsh, ragged breath and felt part of her die inside. Half of her said it was a good thing, but the other half was totally devastated.

'This evening was supposed to turn out very differently,' he continued. 'I was hoping we would have something to celebrate; instead it's turned into a disaster.'

'Oh, no, it's a celebration indeed.' Caron stretched her lips into a facsimile of a smile and, picking up her wine glass, held it aloft. 'A toast, I think, to your departure. It's the best news I've heard in a long time.'

Lawson looked at her long and hard. 'Do you really mean that, Caron?'

How could she lie when she felt so desolate? Suddenly her brave façade crumbled. 'No, I suppose not,' she admitted. 'That wasn't a very nice thing for me to say. Actually I think it's still too soon for you to leave.'

He shook his head. 'The holiday season is drawing to a close and once John's married he won't want me

around, nor, by your admission, will he want you. It
was...' he paused a moment as if wondering whether
to go on, then continued with what looked like great
difficulty '...my intention tonight to ask you if you'd
like to come home with me to Dublin.'

Caron turned startled eyes on his face. 'I beg your
pardon?' *Go home with him*? Her heart began a dra-
matic tattoo within her breast. *Go home with him*? Was
he serious?

'I know we haven't exactly been the best of friends
but in a way we're kindred spirits.'

'If you're talking about the fact that we've both been
let down, then yes, I suppose we are,' she agreed, still
completely bemused by his unexpected suggestion.

'Neither of us wants to settle into a serious relationship, but you cannot deny that in one respect we
feel right together.'

'Right together?' echoed Caron. 'If you mean sexual
attraction, I don't call that feeling right together. I find
that a problem, a very big one. What is it exactly that
you're proposing?'

'I'm giving you the chance of a roof over your head,
a comfortable home, friendship, companionship, and a
lover if you need one.'

'You're not serious?' She did not know what to make
of this unexpected proposal.

'I'm extremely serious,' he told her calmly.

'And what would you get out of it?' Her tone was
sharper than she intended. It was one of her wildest
dreams come true but there had to be some hidden
motive. He wouldn't simply ask her out of the kindness
of his heart.

'I'm not being mercenary, Caron. I don't want anything you're not prepared to give.'

She shook her head. 'It wouldn't work. I wouldn't be happy. It would be wrong for me to live with a man I wasn't married to.' Loving him as she did, knowing he felt nothing for her in return, would be far too painful. She could not even think why he had asked her.

'Then there is only one solution,' he said softly. 'We'll have to get married.'

CHAPTER SEVEN

IT WAS many minutes before Caron could summon up a response to Lawson's astonishing proposal. Marriage! The last thing she had expected—the most bizarre—and yet the most wonderful! Her heart leapt in response then plumbed the depths. Her love for him was so intense that it hurt and the thought of life without him painful. Yet how could it work? What devil had driven him to suggest such a thing?

'You have to be joking?'

He had been carefully monitoring her reaction, seeing the joy she had been unable to hide, the despair, the hope and frustration. 'I'm perfectly serious, Caron.'

'But—but—you——'

'Always said I would never get married?' he finished for her.

Caron nodded, her mouth dry, her throat contracting painfully.

'I've changed my mind. I need a woman in my life.'

'For what?' she asked bitterly. 'To fulfil your physical needs? There are plenty about who'd be only too willing to oblige. You don't have to go to the trouble of getting married.'

'Would you let me make love to *you* out of wedlock?' he asked pointedly.

Caron shook her head. 'You know I wouldn't.' And then frowned. 'Are you saying that—no, I don't believe it. You're willing to marry me just so that you can make love to me? That's the craziest thing I've ever heard. You're as bad as Karl.'

'Heavens, Caron, that's not the reason. I just happen to think that it could work. I think we'd be good company for each other. You have to admit that we've got on well together these last few weeks. You'd have a good life, I'm not a poor man. It would be better than living somewhere on your own, becoming a dried up old spinster before you knew it.'

It wasn't a pleasant picture that he painted, but Caron was not sure that companionship was enough. She loved Lawson with every fibre of her being and wanted him to love her too. She did not want simply to be his house-keeper and his lover. She wanted him emotionally and spiritually as well as physically. 'What sort of commitment would I be giving you? Would I be free to go out with other friends?'

'Male friends?' he barked, so fiercely that he made her jump.

'No, not in the sense you're thinking, anyway. But with such an unconventional marriage surely you wouldn't expect me to sit at home all day and every day like a dutiful wife? And what if it didn't work out—would I be free to leave? Would you divorce me easily or would you insist on our remaining married for the rest of our lives?'

'You could go,' he answered, though his tone was quiet and it was obvious he hoped it would never come to that.

Caron found it difficult to understand his motives. 'I'd like time to think about it,' she said. 'You've taken me completely by surprise.'

'I'll wash up while you think,' he said, abruptly getting up.

'But I don't mean that—I meant—I wanted—I need...'
Her voice trailed off. What was the point? She already
knew what her answer was going to be. She sat and
watched him as he stacked the plates and took them out
into the kitchen.

It was obviously companionship that he sought as well
as a lover. He did not relish the idea of returning to an
empty house. But did she like the idea of going there
either? Would there be too many things to remind her
of Josie? Or had everything been erased on the day that
he'd thrown her out?

But God, how she loved him, and why shouldn't she
take this chance? It could be no worse than going their
separate ways. It could even be better. She made up her
mind there and then that she would win his love, come
what may. It would be a gigantic task, maybe an impossible one, but she was determined to do her best to
prove to him that she was nothing like the women who
had corrupted his mind and ruined his life.

'Well?' The last plate dried and put away, he re-entered
the dining-room and took his seat opposite her.

It was a strange marriage proposal. Lawson looked as
serious as though he were arranging a business deal.

She found herself saying yes while at the same time
her mind was telling her no. You'll live to regret it, Caron,
warned her conscience. He wants to marry you for all
the wrong reasons. Which she knew, of course, but it
seemed to be making no difference. Her voice had accepted on her behalf.

'Good.' His eyes met and locked into hers for a few
vibrating seconds. 'I think we should get married straight
away.'

*   *   *

John was surprised and delighted and if he wondered about the suddenness of it all he said nothing. The wedding took place in the register office a week later. Lawson had given her the choice of a church wedding but she turned it down. In the circumstances it seemed hypocritical. She had not even worn white. Instead she had chosen an ivory two-piece with a small hat and a veil that just covered her eyes. Lawson had worn a new grey suit.

She had actually felt very proud to stand beside him as his wife, and it was the hardest thing in the world to stop the love shining in her eyes. But Lawson had been solemn and withdrawn, his kiss obligatory. From the time he had asked her to marry him to the moment they met in the register office at nine o'clock on Friday morning she had rarely seen him; it was as though he had deliberately kept out of her way. If she had not been so convinced that her love could win through she would have told him to forget the whole thing. She could not understand why he was acting like this.

There had been no reception, just the four of them back at John's house, where their future had been toasted in champagne. She hated to think what her new husband's brother would say when he found out that Lawson had remarried without telling him. But he had wanted everything done quickly and with the minimum of fuss. The arrangements had been made with the precision of an army manoeuvre.

She had telephoned her mother in the Scilly Isles, who had been delighted by the news, but hadn't felt up to making the journey. She suffered badly from arthritis and rarely ventured far from the house which she now shared with her sister. 'You must bring Lawson to see me,' she said, and Caron had promised.

Now they were on their way to Lawson's home in the southern suburbs of Dublin. They spoke of mundane matters only and although the heavy wedding-ring on her finger told her that her status had changed she did not feel married.

She had hoped for more than this. She had thought that once she became Mrs Lawson Savage his demeanour would change. Instead an even bigger gap had opened up between them. She stole a glance at his grim profile, at the hawk-like nose and tight mouth, at the dark hair curling so close to his head. She loved him dearly and yet he was a stranger. Didn't he realise that his attitude was hurting her, that he was making everything so much more difficult?

A tender smile, a caring word, that was all she wanted, something to tell her that she had not made the biggest mistake of her life. 'I know nothing about where you live,' she said, feeling the need to break the enormous silence that had settled over their heads like a raincloud. 'I don't even know what sort of house it is. You haven't told me a thing.'

He looked at her then and she could have been mistaken but she thought he was relieved that she had eased the tension. Perhaps he was as nervous as she about the whole affair? The thought made her feel a bit better and she smiled. 'I trust I won't have to begin cleaning the second I get there.'

She had hoped he would take her away on honeymoon, perhaps to some tropical island where they could really get to know each other, but had not dared make the suggestion herself. When he told her they were going straight to his house she had hidden her disappointment and accepted his decision without demur.

His lips flickered in a mockery of a smile. 'Everything's been attended to, there'll be nothing for you to do. The house itself is virtually brand new, a huge monstrosity in a cul-de-sac with many others. It wasn't my choice.'

No, it had been Josie's, she was aware of that. 'We could sell it and move?' she suggested hopefully. 'Perhaps out into the countryside. Not too far away because of your work, of course.' He had told her that his printing company was in the heart of Dublin. 'But I'd love an old stone cottage.'

His eyes narrowed as he slanted her another glance. 'Are you serious?'

Caron nodded. 'I hated London and its concrete greyness; I often used to wish I'd never moved from Dorset. Our farmhouse was built of stone—it was beautiful.'

He was silent for a moment, but there was no longer the tension that had filled the car earlier. 'My own parents lived in an old cottage in County Wicklow. It was beautiful and peaceful but Josie hated every minute she was there. She wanted to live in the city.'

And so he had given it all up for her. It occurred to Caron that he and Josie had not had very much in common at all. She had obviously been putting on an act when they had first met, having set her sights on him for reasons known only to herself, and not resting until they were married. Only then had the true Josie shown through.

She felt so sorry for him. He'd had more than his share of unhappiness. But that would all change now, she determined, she would do her utmost to please him, she would ensure that every day of his life was filled with enjoyment and love. She would be everything to him that he expected in a woman, warm, loving, sensual. She would derive her pleasure from giving to him.

The house was built of dark red brick which was somewhat unprepossessing, but it was far enough apart from its neighbours not to be overlooked. It was much bigger than Caron had expected, with a wide drive and immaculate lawns, and she could not wait to see inside.

The hall was like a room in itself, and on an oak chest with carved front panels a bowl of freshly cut roses spilled their scent into the air. Caron wondered who had looked after the house and thought of this welcoming touch. Above the chest was a painting of water-lilies which was surely a Monet? Caron knew a little about art, having spent many hours in London's art galleries when she had once been going out with a boy who was passionately interested in painting.

It was warm indoors and she took off her jacket and draped it carelessly over a chair, wandering from room to room. Each was furnished and decorated beautifully, though in a more modern style than Caron liked herself. Nor were there any more paintings by old masters. She decided the Monet was Lawson's choice, the other modern pictures Josie's, chosen simply because they went with the colour of the room.

The kitchen was the only room which appealed to her. It had every modern appliance imaginable with plenty of work surfaces and cupboard space. Caron looked around her in true delight. 'Lawson, this is fantastic. We had an old-fashioned kitchen at the farmhouse, and a cubby-hole of a kitchen at my London flat—which I used to share with two other girls—so this is like heaven. I'm going to love cooking here.' She peeped into cupboards and the fridge and the freezer and everything was full.

Lawson raised a brow at her enthusiasm. 'Don't get too carried away; I have a housekeeper who does most of the cooking.'

'A housekeeper?' Caron felt her initial pleasure fade.

'That's right. When Josie—er—left, I needed someone to look after the house.'

'But—I'll be able to do all that now. You won't need anyone else,' she protested. It would ruin everything with another woman in the house. She needed Lawson to herself so that she could work on him.

'Mrs Blake is indispensable,' he told her gruffly. 'Besides, she needs the money. She has a daughter in a— in—hospital—the same place where Emily was—and it costs her a small fortune in travelling expenses.'

Caron understood immediately. What a big heart this man had—and what a great pity that life had been such a disillusionment. It made her all the more determined to prove to him that not everyone in the world was uncaring.

'Where is Mrs Blake now?' she asked.

'Probably at the hospital.'

'Will she be back later?'

'I doubt it. We probably won't see her until the morning.'

'She doesn't sleep here, then?'

Lawson shook his head and Caron felt relieved, though she did not know why.

Upstairs he showed her the five bedrooms, each one with its own bathroom, each one with a different colour scheme. 'This was mine and Josie's,' he told her thickly, then shut the door again before she'd had more than a glimpse of pink feminine frills and ornate gilt-framed mirrors. Caron was glad they weren't going to sleep in there. She did not want to have to fight memories as well.

'I thought we'd use this one.' It was not such a large room and was decorated in peach and grey and white. Again it wasn't exactly Caron's style, and nor did she believe it was Lawson's.

He had already put their cases at the foot of the bed but it was the bed itself with its boldly patterned quilt that held Caron's eyes and she realised that it was here that Lawson would make love to her for the first time. She swallowed hard and attempted to back out of the room but he stood right behind her. 'What's wrong? Does the thought of our sharing that bed disturb you?' His hands encircled her waist and he drew her back against him.

'Of course not.' Excite was the word, not disturb. It was beginning already with the feel of his hard-muscled body against her, his hands stroking and promising untold pleasures. For so long she had wanted him to make love to her and now it was going to happen and she would be able to give free rein to her feelings. It would be the culmination of all her dreams and she hoped that her inexperience would not be a disappointment to him. What happened today would set the standard. It was important that they were completely compatible in this direction, thus making it easier for her to work on him in other ways.

'Good,' he growled, 'because tonight our marriage will be consummated in that bed, make no bones about it.' His hands moved slowly and tormentingly upwards over her stomach and her ribcage, finally, possessively, capturing her breasts.

Caron drew in a sharp breath, feeling them harden and ache with pleasure and need, and at the same time feeling Lawson's own undisguised arousal. She wanted to twist round in his arms and offer her mouth up for his kisses and beg him to take her to bed now.

His fingers teased and tortured through the silk of her blouse. The thin material felt like an iron-clad barrier and she wanted to tear it off and feel the abrasiveness of his fingers against the scented softness of her bare skin.

'I have no intention of denying you anything, Lawson,' she whispered as her head fell back against his shoulder. 'I entered into this marriage with my eyes wide open.'

Her words caused his hands to tighten on her breasts and she knew that, given the encouragement, he would take her there and then. But she did not want him to think that she was giving in too easily and she twisted away from him with a rueful little smile. 'The only thing that's bothering me is what I'm going to do with myself all day long while you're out at work. I imagine your housekeeper won't want me interfering.'

'I'm sure a woman of your intellect will be able to find plenty to keep you occupied.' He moved with her and stroked the tips of his fingers over her breasts, featherlight touches designed to let her know that she wasn't going to get away from him as easily as that. 'Redecorate the whole house if you like. Josie had some interior designers in—all this was to her taste, not mine. If you want to change anything feel free. In fact I'd welcome it.'

Caron edged away from him again, refusing to look into the intoxicating warmth of his eyes. She had never been let loose to do any decorating before. What if she made mistakes? 'I suppose I could do it,' she said, careful not to sound too happy even though the thought was tremendously exciting. 'But what if you don't like my choice either? Shouldn't it be something we decide together?'

'You can't do any worse than Josie,' he said dismissively. 'I really won't have time to bother myself with it. Go ahead and do what you like.'

Caron felt a surge of relief when he left the room without touching her again. It was going to be difficult convincing him that she was a reluctant lover when she ached with a consuming passion that only he could assuage. She found it difficult to believe that she had never felt like this with Karl. She had been so convinced that he was the right man for her. It just went to show that she did not always know what was best.

Slowly she unpacked both his and her own clothes. Not that he had very much, just the few items he had bought since the fire. But there were suits and shirts galore in one of the wardrobes, making it obvious that he had slept in this room after Josie left.

For a few moments she stood and looked around, trying to picture his dark head and her blonde one on the pillow. Which side of the bed would he sleep on? Did he wear pyjamas or nothing but his birthday suit? Her cheeks flushed prettily at the thought. There was a whole new world to be explored that was both disturbing and stimulating at the same time.

She took a shower in the adjoining bathroom and put her toothbrush in the holder next to his. Such intimacy was new to her and yet it felt good to be sharing Lawson's home with him. If it didn't work out it certainly wouldn't be for want of trying.

Maybe she could cook them a meal, she thought, as she made her way down to the kitchen. They could eat it in the pretty green dining-room. This time she would put candles on the table and pretend they had married for all the right reasons.

'What are you doing?'

Lawson's deep, spine-tingling voice came over her shoulder as she peered into the refrigerator.

She turned and met the deep blue of his eyes, which as always sent shivers of sensation through her veins. 'I'm wondering what I can cook for our supper? I don't know about you but I'm starving.'

'And you think I would allow you to cook on your wedding day?' His tone held just a hint of dry humour.

Caron shrugged with what she hoped was the right show of indifference. 'It's no ordinary marriage.' And he had said *her* wedding day, not *ours*. The omission hurt.

'Even so, you shouldn't be cooking,' he admonished. 'We can either eat out or I'll send for something. I know a very good firm who specialise in dinners for two. It's delivered piping hot, complete with champagne and candles and flowers. Would you like that? Or would that be the wrong thing to do as well, considering this is "no ordinary marriage"?' There was a sudden cutting edge to his voice.

Caron squirmed inside. She had not realised he would object to her words, even though they were the truth. She eyed him guardedly. 'Perhaps we'd better eat out.' The sort of meal he had described could prove disastrous in the circumstances.

She was glad that she had changed into a dress that was rather special. In a soft pearl-grey lightweight jersey, it was clinging but not too much so. It was high-necked and long-sleeved, yet sexy in a subtle sort of way.

While she fetched her bag he phoned the restaurant and it was just a short drive away. It was a nice place and the food excellent but Lawson knew too many people and Caron felt it might have been better if they had eaten at home after all.

She was the subject of much speculation and gossip throughout the whole evening, and one girl, a beautiful girl with jet-black hair and scarlet lips, paused at their table and asked Lawson where Josie was. In other words did his wife know he was out with another woman?

Caron could not believe her audacity and held her breath as she waited for his answer, seeing the furious emotion build up inside him. 'Haven't you heard, my wife died?' he told her with superhuman restraint.

As the girl's eyes began to light up Caron lifted her hand with its brand-new wedding-ring. 'And I'm the new Mrs Lawson Savage,' she told her pointedly.

Heavily pencilled brows rose, then, with a delicate shrug and a few muttered words, the girl turned and left.

'I hadn't realised you were so popular. Shall I have to fend off many such admirers?' Caron asked with a smile, hoping her jealousy did not shine through. 'There are still one or two looking at you across the room.' It appeared that half the female population of Dublin were in love with him—and who could blame them with his dark good looks and powerful personality? Perhaps one of the reasons he had married her was to protect himself from such predatory females.

'I imagine Caroline will spread the word,' he said gruffly.

'I presume she knew nothing about your divorce?'

'It wasn't something that I broadcast—I wasn't particularly proud of it. No man likes to think that he's not capable of keeping his wife satisfied.' A muscle jerked in his jaw as he spoke. 'I think it's time we left.'

Caron's stomach worked nervously on the way home. The time was fast drawing near when they would share the handsome bed in the peach and grey room and she was not sure that she would be able to handle it.

She was relieved and surprised when he led the way into the sitting-room and suggested a nightcap. French windows looked out over the garden and at the flick of a switch the whole area was illuminated with strategically placed lamps. There was no need for a light in the sitting-room itself; the gentle glow from outside filtered in, making it feel as though they were a part of it.

There was a pool with a fountain, a terrace with lots of tubs and urns filled with geraniums and ivy and other flowering plants, lawns leading away into the black distance where the lights did not reach. It was difficult to believe that they were on the outskirts of the grey city of Dublin.

Caron sat on a couch near to the window and drank it all in. 'This is lovely,' she said. 'It's a pity it's not warm enough to sit outside. Did you design all this yourself?'

'No,' he confessed brusquely. 'Josie called in a firm of landscape gardeners.'

Josie had done a good job of spending his money, she thought bitterly. Was that why she had married him—because he was rich? Caron realised that she actually knew very little about Lawson's financial affairs. He had told her that he was not a poor man but it really made no difference to her. She loved him for who he was, not for the size of his bank balance.

'It's a little too artificial for my liking,' he growled. 'I prefer cottage gardens full of old-fashioned flowers.'

How alike they were, thought Caron, as she took her drink from him, and felt acutely disappointed when he did not sit on the couch beside her but instead deliberately chose a chair a few feet away. She felt hurt but tried not to show it, instead looking speculatively at the expensive crystal glass half-filled with pale amber liquid.

'Whiskey and dry,' he told her in such a tone that suggested if she did not like it, too bad. His own whiskey he drank neat.

'I think,' she said, after they had sat for a minute or two in uncomfortable silence, 'that we ought to tell your brother we're married.' She watched his reaction closely and did not miss the sudden tightening of his lips. In the orange glow from the outdoor lamps his skin looked like polished teak, the angles of his face more accented, and when he looked at her his eyes were as black as night.

'There's plenty of time for that. Once Stephanie and Bruce know they'll be trooping over here to congratulate us. I think we should give ourselves time to settle in.'

Caron lifted her shoulders. 'Personally I'd be very hurt if my brother got married without telling me.' But not as hurt as she was now. Since the dark-haired Caroline's untimely reminder of his wife he had again distanced himself from her. Was he regretting the impulse that had made him propose marriage? Was he already fearing that it was not the right solution? It was up to her to make him feel better but how was she going to do that when he had erected a brick wall ten feet thick around himself?

'Bruce will understand,' he said gruffly.

'You mean he'll guess that our marriage isn't a love match?'

His eyes flashed contemptuously. 'Of course. He knows how strongly I feel about women in general. It would have to be someone with very special qualities to make me change my mind.'

Meaning she hadn't got them, thought Caron, dangerously close to tears. Although she had known it when she had agreed to marry him, it hurt all the same. 'So what will he think when he finds out?'

Lawson shrugged. 'He can think what the hell he likes. What I do is my own affair. Drink up.'

Caron took another sip of her whiskey and lapsed into silence. This evening was going nothing like what she had expected. When Lawson had embraced her in the bedroom she had thought it was a taste of things to come. She had envisaged a very active physical relationship, because despite his denial she felt sure that was the main reason he had married her. And yet now he was cold and remote and it was difficult to imagine any sort of relationship at all.

Was it a sign of things to come? Would he be one moment passionate and intense, the next, cold and withdrawn? Would she be able to handle it? She gulped another mouthful of whiskey, finishing it off and placing the glass on a small side-table.

Suddenly she did not want to go to bed; she was afraid of the outcome. She could not stand the thought that he might lie still and silent and ignore her. On the other hand instant lovemaking was out of the question as well. Surely he must know that his restraint was in no way conducive to making love?

'I'll wash the glasses,' she said when he finished his own drink and stood up. Instead of looking forward to sharing Lawson's bed she was now dreading it.

'Mrs Blake will do them in the morning,' he told her crisply.

'But I don't mind, really I don't.'

'It's what she's paid for,' he barked. 'What is this, have you suddenly got cold feet? Did you hope that if

I went to bed first I might be asleep before you came up? Nothing's changed, Caron, nor will it. You're my woman now, in every sense of the word.'

Caron shivered and wondered what she had let herself in for. She had been too blinded by her own love to see any further than the fact that her body craved his. She had envisaged a two-sided affair, both of them needing and wanting each other with the same intensity of feeling. She had expected and needed warmth and a show of caring, not this basic animal hunger and the suggestion that he was going to take her whether she wanted it or not.

'Of course I haven't forgotten,' she whispered huskily. 'I'm not used to having a housekeeper, that's all. I've always had to do these sort of things for myself.'

'Not any longer,' he growled and, flicking out the light, he headed for the stairs.

By the time they reached the bedroom Caron's heart was racing fit to burst. It felt so loud in her ears that she was sure Lawson must hear it too and guess at her panic. She had no idea what was going to happen next, except that he intended to consummate their marriage, but at what cost to her?

She risked a glance at him and there was no softening of his features, his face was still all harsh lines and angles. She turned away and fled into the bathroom, standing behind the door for a few trembling moments before brushing her teeth and washing off her make-up. This wasn't what she had expected, this wasn't the way she had envisaged things at all. She could not, would not let Lawson make love to her while he was in such a terrible mood.

When she came out he had undressed right down to his underpants and her eyes were drawn to him like a magnet, seeing again the hard, flat stomach and impressively muscled chest with its covering of dark hairs which arrowed downwards, the long powerful legs which had taken him through the forest with the easy loping gait of a tiger.

There was definitely something of the animal in him tonight—in his relaxed yet threatening stance, in the glitter of his eyes, the impression he gave of being ready and waiting for the inevitable.

As she circled away from the bathroom door he circled towards it, neither taking their eyes off the other, reminding her of two animals sizing each other up for the fray.

The second he was inside the bathroom she ripped off her own clothes and pulled on her nightdress, diving beneath the quilt with the energy and skill of an acrobat. He might have no qualms about her seeing him naked but she had no wish to be ogled.

She heard the shower running, which gave her a few more unexpected minutes of freedom, and when he came out of the bathroom her eyes were tightly closed.

'It's no use pretending you're asleep.' His voice had lost its hard edge, as though he had washed his anger away with the steaming jets of water. Instead it was filled with mockery and she sensed him walking round to her side of the bed instead of his own.

'I'm not pretending anything.' She opened her eyes and then tensed inside as she saw him standing over her in all his full naked glory. She wanted to shut her lids again quickly but that would give away the fact that he disturbed her, so she looked up boldly into his face and ventured a faint smile.

'You're waiting for me?'

She swallowed hard and nodded.

'Good, because I've been waiting for you for a very long time. And I have no intention of letting you hide your tantalising little body beneath a quilt. I want to see what I'm getting for my money.' The duvet was whipped off her almost before he had finished speaking, certainly before Caron had absorbed his meaning.

His eyes narrowed when he saw her nightdress. 'What's this?' he asked tauntingly. 'Another barrier? Were you expecting me to leave you alone?'

'I didn't doubt for one minute that you wouldn't carry out your threat,' she retorted, sitting up now and hugging her knees to her chest.

'Threat? Is that how you see it?' His voice was suddenly harsh again. 'It was no threat, I assure you, it was a promise. It's what you've wanted for as long as I have. Deny it if you dare.'

'I thought,' she flashed, 'when I agreed to marry you, that making love would be a beautiful experience. I didn't realise that I would be subjected to—to humiliation like this.'

'Caron.' He walked around the bed and climbed on the other side. 'It has never been my intention to threaten or humiliate you, and you need not fear that I shall hurt you. But lesson number one before we go any further is that you relax and learn to trust me.'

He moved closer so that their bodies were touching and she saw in his eyes the hunger of love and knew there and then that it was going to happen tonight just the way he had said. She knew also that she would not fight him, that she would weakly surrender her body to his as soon as he began his assault.

When he touched his fingertips to her throat, sliding them down its length, finding the tell-tale pulse beating erratically at its base, she knew nothing mattered any more. Already she could feel the tension going out of her and a response welling up inside, and when, slowly, oh, so slowly, he eased her nightdress up over her head, she offered no resistance at all.

His eyes burned a trail of sensation as they raked every inch of her naked body, from the tips of her pink-painted toenails to the firmness of her breasts, where already her nipples were hard and excited. When his hands began to follow the same path Caron forgot everything except her need for him. She could feel hot liquid running through her veins, excitement so intense that it hurt.

'You're beautiful, quite, quite beautiful,' he told her hoarsely, his hands sliding over her shoulders and breasts then down over her ribcage and the flatness of her stomach and the curve of her hips. There was not an inch of her body that he was not exploring.

She had unconsciously slipped down the bed again, and was feasting her eyes on this man who was awakening sensations that she had never felt before. Who would have believed that such a light touch could set her on fire, could cause a definite ache in her groin and her breasts, and a longing for ultimate fulfilment?

She felt no shyness, no embarrassment, and when he lay down alongside her, when she felt his skin searing her own skin, she almost cried out her pleasure. And then his mouth was on hers and her response was instant, the floodgates were opened on the tide of desire that had been threatening to flood through her for so very long.

His hand touched her breast, his thumb brushing the nipple, causing exquisite sensations and making her ache inside with very real need.

'Lawson.' His name was dragged from the depths of her throat, her eyes unusually dark as she looked at him, wondering at the feelings that were building up inside her, feelings that this man, who did not even love her, was managing to arouse.

'My beautiful Caron.' He traced the outline of her lips with a sensitive finger, feeling their soft fullness and the way they trembled beneath his touch. 'Do not be afraid, I promise not to hurt you.' There was a raw quality to his voice that was in complete contrast to the harshness and anger she was so used to.

Caron marvelled at her new-found desires. She had never known how strong they could be, had never guessed that she was capable of such potent emotions, and when he took one aching nipple into his mouth such sensations as she had never experienced before shuddered through every inch of her body.

Her hands went to his head, her fingers threading through the thickness of his hair, holding him to her. He transferred his mouth to her other breast, sucking deeply, making her cry out with pleasure and desire, her hands on his back now, her nails digging into his skin.

She could not stop the animal whimpers that were escaping her throat, or the tremors of wild sensation that pulsed through her veins. She felt alive, vibrantly alive, more alive than she had ever felt in her life. She had been afraid that Lawson would take her without her being ready for him but it was not like that at all. She wanted him now, she did not want to wait, she did not want him to prolong his assault, and without even realising what she was doing Caron arched her body into him, telling him, willing him, pleading with him.

Against her she felt his arousal; even so he was in no hurry to comply with her demands. His mouth left her breasts to burn a slow trail over her stomach, his fingers exploring her intimately. She was lost in a world of raging senses and driving need and when he finally entered her she cried out her pleasure.

Feverish hunger and wild and beautiful sensations raged through her. Nothing had prepared her for anything like this. She felt awed that her body was receiving him so easily, as though it had been waiting for this very moment all her adult life. Making love with Karl paled into insignificance beside it. She felt as though she was soaring as high as an eagle.

And then came the unexpected explosion of sensation which spiralled out from the very heart of her to reach every corner of her body, sending after it shock wave after shock wave of feeling more intense than she had ever thought possible.

Lawson too was gripped in an emotion that made his body tremble and surge. Deep guttural sounds of anguish came from his throat as his fingers dug into her flesh and long after he lay spent at her side deep shudders racked through him.

Caron felt incapable of moving. Never had she expected to feel anything like this. Every ounce of strength had gone out of her and all she wanted to do was lie in the curve of Lawson's arm. It had been a mind-blowing experience and she felt sure now that everything was going to be all right. With a satisfied smile on her lips she fell asleep.

When Caron awoke the room was awash with sunlight. She felt warm and comfortable and discovered that the quilt was back over her but the bed at her side was empty. She reached out and it was cold, as though Lawson had been missing for a long time, and the thought sliced through her with painful clarity that he had left her side the instant she had fallen asleep—after taking what he wanted!

CHAPTER EIGHT

BITTERNESS seared through Caron as she pulled on a cotton housecoat and went looking for Lawson. Last night had been such a beautiful experience that she did not want to believe he had deserted her like this, did not want to believe that it meant nothing to him, that he had been using her just as she had feared all along.

There was no sign of him anywhere though she found a lukewarm coffee-pot in the kitchen. Why hadn't he woken her? Why hadn't he at least left a note? It was eight o'clock. Where had he gone at this hour?

The questions rushed around unanswered inside Caron's mind as she retraced her steps to the bedroom. Feeling numb inside, all of the warm feelings that had still been with her when she awoke gone, she showered and dressed and went back downstairs.

She made fresh coffee and sat at the breakfast-bar drinking it. Was it always going to be like this? Was he going to use her body when the mood took him but ignore her for the rest of the time? How could she cope if that were so? She had sworn to herself that she would treat him with warmth and love and friendship, show him that she was different from other women, but how could she do it if this was how he was going to behave?

When she heard the door open she turned with a hesitant smile and a quickening of her heartbeats. Maybe he had some perfectly plausible reason for going out. She could be getting all worked up for nothing.

The woman who stood there was plump and middle-aged with lines of worry scoured on her face but at this moment a warm smile on her lips. 'Mrs—Savage?' she enquired, looking with interest at Caron.

Caron nodded and smiled back. 'And you must be Mrs Blake?' Disappointment that it was not Lawson welled up inside her.

'That's right, dearie. Lawson phoned and told me you were still in bed. Said I wasn't to wake you. But since you're up I'll cook your breakfast. I take it you haven't eaten?'

'No, I haven't.' Caron hated the thought that he had got in touch with his housekeeper instead of telling her where he was going, only slightly mollified by the fact that he had not wanted her disturbed. 'But I'm not really hungry,' she added. 'Where is Lawson?'

'He's gone to the office, didn't he tell you last night?' The woman's thin brows rose in surprise. 'Poor man, the instant he's home and he's back at work. Not much of a honeymoon for you, though, is it? But I've no doubt he'll take you somewhere nice later on when he's caught up with things here.'

The joke of the century, thought Caron sourly. She was fast discovering that their marriage wasn't the sort that demanded a honeymoon, or any other niceties that usually went along with being a new bride. If the truth were known he was treating her as a whore and she ought to have realised that from the onset and never gone along with his monstrous proposal.

'I can understand why he felt the need to hide himself away,' went on Mrs Blake. 'He was terribly cut up when his sister died, and coming on top of his divorce I didn't think he was going to get over it. But things will be different now, I'm sure, and of course you must eat. How about some scrambled eggs on toast and a nice pot of tea? I'll bring it to you in the sitting-room. It's nice in there, you can look out at the garden and watch the birds while you eat.'

'That would be very nice,' answered Caron. 'Thank you.' She wondered whether Mrs Blake was always this talkative. 'But you don't have to wait on me, I can make my own breakfast.' It was very clear that Lawson was the apple of the woman's eye and could do no wrong.

'No, no, you mustn't do that,' tutted the housekeeper. 'It's what I'm here for, and a very generous employer Lawson is, too. You've married a wonderful man, I can't sing his praises loud enough.'

It was evident she had seen only one side to his character, thought Caron irately. She would have the shock of her life if she knew how he was treating her.

To her surprise Caron managed to eat all of her breakfast but she could not help feeling resentful that Lawson had thought his work more important than her. They at least could have had the weekend together before he went back. She could understand his wanting to see what had been happening in his absence, but at this hour—and on the day after he had got married?

She did not even have any idea what time Lawson planned on coming back. The more she thought about his absence, the angrier she became. How dared he do this to her? Hadn't she pleased him last night? Had her lack of experience been a complete turn-off? Hadn't he been able to wait to get away from her?

Shaking her head savagely, she wondered if this was going to be the way of things to come, he leading his own life, she hers. He had promised her a roof over her head and that was about all he was giving her—there was certainly no affection of any sort. 'Redecorate the house,' he had said, 'if you're bored,' but how wasteful that would be when everything was in such good decorative order.

Admittedly she would have liked to change some of the colour schemes and put large comfortable settees in the lounge instead of the angular chairs which were surely not made to be sat on for very long. But it would all take a lot of money and she had been brought up to be prudent.

Mrs Blake went home after lunch, having first prepared their evening meal. All Caron had to do was pop it into the oven. 'I'll see you on Monday, dearie, I shall be at the hospital all day tomorrow visiting my daughter. Just let me know if there's any food you particularly like. Lawson's always been easygoing, eating anything I put in front of him, but I know you might have your likes and dislikes, so I won't be offended if you tell me.'

In one way it was a relief when she had gone, on the other hand the house became dreadfully quiet. Caron walked out into the garden and sat on a bench overlooking the pool. Fat goldfish moved lazily beneath glossy green water-lily leaves the size of dinner plates, peaceful and content in their watery world. No problems for them, no difficulties with relationships.

Caron had the meal cooked and the table laid by six, but at seven Lawson had still not come home. If she had known where to contact him she would have telephoned, but he had never mentioned the name of his printing company, all she knew was that it was somewhere in the city. It made her realise how little she knew about him.

It was eight-thirty when he finally arrived and there was no word of apology for going out and neglecting her. In fact the first thing he did was pour himself a glass of whiskey. Caron had been ready to rant and rave because of the dinner that was very nearly ruined, but when she saw how tired and drawn he was she felt compassion instead.

'You look as though you've had a hard day,' she said softly. 'Have things been left to slide while you were away? Perhaps I could come to the office and help if it's that bad? I am an experienced secretary after all; there must be something I can do.'

'Everything is in perfect order,' he told her coolly, 'I don't need any help. But naturally I want to familiarise myself with everything that's been going on.'

'And it couldn't wait until Monday?' she asked, trying to sound reasonable, hurt by his unexpected coldness towards her. 'Surely it wasn't necessary to go in today?'

'I personally thought it was,' he answered brusquely.

'The least you could have done was woken me and told me what you'd planned,' she protested mildly. 'Until Mrs Blake arrived I had no idea what had happened to you.'

'And it worried you, did it?' he asked harshly.

What had she done to deserve such treatment? Caron wondered. His angry tone rankled, made her say words she did not mean. 'Indeed not, why should it?' Her tone was sharp now, her chin defiant.

Lawson's eyes narrowed. 'That doesn't sound very much like a newlywed.'

'A newlywed?' Her green eyes flashed contemptuously. 'This is a marriage with a difference and you're certainly reminding me of it. You go your way, I go mine. That's it, isn't it? The only time we meet is in bed. I thought in the beginning that you wanted me to look after your house as well, and perhaps needed a companion; now I'm actually wondering why it is you ever asked me to marry you.'

'I thought it would be to our mutual advantage. Obviously I was wrong,' he snarled.

At this rate they could go on arguing all night, thought Caron. It might be as well to back down before things became too ugly. 'Why don't you shower and change?' she asked, her tone softer. 'Dinner's in the oven. You must be starving.'

'No, thanks,' he said gruffly. 'I had a sandwich at the office.'

'Mrs Blake prepared it; she won't be happy if she knows her good cooking's gone to waste.'

'Perhaps later,' he muttered, getting up and pouring himself another generous measure of whiskey.

He had never drunk much before and Caron wondered what was wrong now that he felt the need for it? Was it because of her? Was he already regretting his decision to marry her? She felt desolate inside and needed to find out what was wrong.

'Is it because of last night that you're angry with me? Didn't I come up to your expectations?' she asked bitterly. 'I know I'm unpractised in the art of making love, but——'

'Last night has nothing to do with it,' he interjected crisply. 'I—no—forget it.' His face closed. 'I'll go up and take that shower.' He finished his drink in one swallow and headed for the stairs.

Caron felt bemused but it was no use pondering. There was no way she could guess what he had been going to say. She checked the table, which she had set earlier, and when Lawson came down she had everything ready.

But it was a mockery of a meal. Lawson ate hardly anything and although she had been hungry when he came home she now found that she had lost her own appetite as well. Even her attempts at conversation fell flat. 'You didn't warn me that Mrs Blake was so talkative,' met with nothing more than a grunt. And 'It seems a shame to repaper these walls when there's nothing wrong with them,' merited the response,

'It's up to you.'

It was obvious he had no interest at all in the house, thought Caron, and with hindsight she realised it had been a mistake coming here at all. They would have done much better to set up home in a place that held no memories. Perhaps that was what was wrong. Perhaps all the time he saw Josie and was reminded of her perfidy? It had been wrong to argue with him; she should have held her tongue and been warm and understanding. Hadn't she promised herself that she would do everything possible to change his opinion of women, and hadn't she just been guilty of doing the very opposite? From now on she would be different.

'What shall we do tomorrow?' she asked with enforced cheerfulness, getting up to clear the table.

'You can do what you like,' he told her bluntly, 'I'm going to the office again.'

Caron was stunned. 'But, Lawson, it's Sunday. You can't work on a Sunday.'

'I'll work any day I damn well like,' he told her brutally.

She swallowed a hard lump in her throat. 'Do you think it's being fair on me?' she asked quietly.

'I've told you, find yourself something to do around the house.'

'And I've told you it doesn't need anything doing to it. It would be a complete waste of money replacing things that have years of life left in them.'

'I can afford it.'

'I've never wasted a penny in my life, Lawson Savage, and I have no intention of starting now.' Again her voice had risen and again she cursed herself for not being more in control of her feelings.

He looked at her for several long seconds, as if seeing her clearly for the very first time. 'You're the only girl I know who hasn't wanted to take me for every penny I've got.'

'And you find that remarkable?' she asked with raised eyebrows. 'Didn't you know that before you married me? I don't covet money, Lawson. A simple life suits me fine.'

'Why didn't I meet you earlier?' he muttered thickly, then swung away from the table and made his way heavily upstairs.

Caron was left staring after him, but with hope rising in her heart. It looked as though her earlier thoughts were right. He was still thinking about Josie and the way she had treated him. But if she waited, if she was patient, then everything would turn out all right in the end.

Although she knew she ought to leave the dishes for Mrs Blake Caron washed up and cleared away, making it last as long as she could, delaying the time when she joined Lawson in their bedroom, the uncertainty of not knowing what to expect making her nervous. But her worries were unfounded. When she got there Lawson was sound asleep.

She undressed and crawled, naked, into bed beside him, her emotions mixed. In one way she was relieved that there was to be no further confrontation, on the other hand it was hard lying next to the man she loved, aching to be held in his arms, yet knowing that his feelings did not match hers.

It was a long time before she fell asleep and when she did she dreamt about Karl Britt. He was pursuing her down a long, unending road, calling her name, declaring he still loved her, wanting to know why she had called an end to their engagement. At the same time six or seven other girls were running after him, all shouting that they loved him and why was he rejecting them?

Every time Caron looked over her shoulder his face loomed closer, distorted as though viewed through a too-close camera lens, and his voice became distorted as well until it was all a mad jumble of pictures and sounds.

And then the girls reached him and began tearing at his clothing, screaming undying love, and Caron took the opportunity to run even faster but no matter how hard she tried she remained in the same spot. Unseen arms held her, stopped her from running away, and she struggled and cried out but it made no difference.

'It's all right, Caron, everything's all right.' The words penetrated her subconscious and she awakened with the realisation that it was Lawson's arms that bound her.

'Relax, Caron, you were dreaming.' His voice was soft and soothing, his hand stroking back the damp hair from her face. 'And, judging by the way you were thrashing about, I suspect it was a nightmare? Care to tell me about it?' He made no effort to let her go and in all truthfulness Caron did not want him to.

'I was trying to get away from Karl,' she murmured, her dream already fading, pleasure in this man's body taking its place. Sensations ran riot through her nerve-ends but as she felt his sudden tension at the mention of the other man's name she added quickly, 'And don't ask me why I dreamt about him. Karl was a jerk. I have no idea why I went out with him in the first place.'

'For the same reason any girl goes out with a member of the opposite sex—because you were attracted to him. And yet he hurt you so much, he made you wary of

entering into any other serious relationships. Some man!'
he added caustically. 'But he must have had a very profound effect for you to dream about him so strongly
after all this time.'

'His callous treatment of me isn't something I can
easily forget,' she admitted, and then wondered what
she was doing talking about Karl when she was being
held in the arms of the man she loved. There was no
comparison between them. Karl was arrogant and big-
headed, conscious of his outstanding good looks and his
attraction to women. He was vain, with an ego the size
of a mountain.

Lawson, on the other hand, although very handsome,
did not give the impression that he was aware of it.
Maybe he was arrogant too, and he could be ruthless,
but she had found out that deep down inside he was a
caring, kind man. It was only a matter of time before
she saw this side of him for herself. All it needed was
the right approach on her behalf.

'It's wrong to let someone like Britt ruin your life.'

'I didn't know he was going to hurt me until it was
too late,' she said defensively, wondering at the same
time exactly why she had dreamt about him. Since
meeting Lawson she had thought about Karl less and
less and knew now that all men weren't the same.

Lawson, on the other hand, was still firmly anti-
women. He would never love again. He might grow to
like her, and indeed be affectionate towards her, but she
doubted she would ever have his unfettered love. And
unless some miracle happened and he told her that he
loved her then she would never reveal her love for him.

The hand that had been stroking her hair moved down
over her shoulders to mould the shape of her breast, the
brush of his thumb sensitising her nipple, causing her

to move with unconscious provocation against him, and before she knew it he was making love to her again.

It was sweet torture feeling him inside her, at the same time knowing that all he was doing was feeding his hunger. Why couldn't he love her as she loved him? Tears of frustration rolled down her cheeks but when Lawson asked her what was wrong Caron shook her head. 'Nothing,' she whispered achingly.

'You don't have to do this if it's not what you want,' he said in sudden anger, withdrawing abruptly from her. 'I'm not such a bastard that I'd force you into anything just because we're now man and wife.'

Caron avoided his eyes. 'It's not that.'

'Then why the tears? Did I hurt you?'

She twisted away from him, drawing herself up into the foetal position, pushing her knuckles into her mouth in an attempt to stop herself from blurting out the truth.

'Caron, answer me.' He took her firmly by the shoulders and turned her so that she was facing him and she could feel his tension as if it were her own.

'You didn't hurt me.' There was a choking lump in her throat that was painful. 'I think I was crying because I—I—' Dear God, what could she say? That it was because she was happy? Because she enjoyed his lovemaking? Because it was the best thing that had ever happened to her? No, every single answer would give her away. 'Dammit, Lawson, I don't have to explain myself.'

He snorted in disgust. 'I'll never understand the vagaries of women. Go back to sleep but don't think you've won. Another night I might not be so generous.'

It was a long, long time before she fell asleep. She hated it when he ignored her; she wanted to be held in his arms and made to feel that she was someone special.

Last night had been wonderful and she wanted to repeat it tonight and every night, and not only in bed but wherever and whenever they felt like making love. Surely that was how marriage should be, a bonding of souls and bodies whenever the mood took them?

Lawson lay still and silent though she knew he was not asleep and she wondered if she ought to try to explain what had happened to her. But without giving away the fact that she was deeply in love with him it was impossible, and to have him throw her love back in her face would hurt far more than putting up with his inconsistent moods. All she could do was enjoy their good moments together and cope with the bad as best she could.

Eventually sleep claimed her and when she awoke the next time it was morning and she had the bed to herself yet again. It did not surprise her but neither did she relish the thought of another long, empty day, without even the loquacious Mrs Blake to break it up. She decided that as soon as she had eaten her breakfast she would go out and explore Dublin city. She had never been before and, like all capitals, it must have many places of interest.

Although she had not eaten much of her meal last night Caron still did not feel very hungry, and, after eating only one slice of buttered toast and drinking two cups of tea, she fetched her bag and her coat and set off.

The sky in the west was pale and promising but overhead the clouds were grey, some of them almost black, and Caron sensed that it would rain before long. She had been lucky in that they'd had very little rain in the few weeks she had been in Ireland. Her brother had told her that it rained more often than not, which accounted for the lush greenness of the countryside.

Surprisingly Dublin reminded her of London. The River Liffey winding through its centre could have been the Thames, the Georgian architecture in the better part of the city was reminiscent of London's West End, the dockland could have been the Thames beyond Tower Bridge, and the double-decker buses only needed to change from green to red to complete the scene.

And then there was the Guinness brewery and more pubs than she had ever seen in her life, confirming what she had been told about the Irish spending most of their time in the pub.

She window-shopped in Grafton Street and made up her mind to come back when the shops were open, she sat on a bench in St Stephen's Green, studied posters outside various theatres, and visited the National Gallery, where she had a sandwich and cup of coffee in the restaurant. After she had done all that, footsore but happier, Caron made her way home.

It was drizzling with rain now but fortunately it had kept off for most of the day. Having walked much further than she had intended, Caron looked forward to a long soak in the bath before preparing their supper. To say she was surprised to find Lawson already home was putting it mildly, but his anger at her absence was even more unexpected.

He yanked the door open before she could insert her key in the lock and looked at her with blazing blue eyes. 'Where the hell have you been?'

Caron frowned. 'Just out.'

'Out where?' he demanded, stepping back for her to enter, slamming the door shut, then standing in front of her with his fingers curled into fists.

'For a walk, that's all. Is there anything wrong in that?' Anger flared inside her too but it subsided just as quickly when it struck her that he was comparing her behaviour with Josie's. But if he thought she had been out looking for other men then he was grossly mistaken. 'Into the city, looking at the sights,' she hastened to add. 'I wish you'd been with me, though, it would have been much more enjoyable.'

'This is only your second day here. Surely you're not sick to death of the house yet?'

'You don't know what it's like to be reminded of your wife everywhere I look,' she protested. It wasn't the exact truth but it was a good enough excuse.

'Haven't I told you to go ahead and change things?' he asked impatiently.

'And I've told you why I won't.'

'Oh, yes,' he snorted, 'sweet words designed to get on the right side of me. And with such impact that I came home much earlier than I'd intended just to be with you.'

Caron drew in a breath of sheer pain. Was that really true? If only she'd known! 'I'm sorry, I had no idea.'

'Of course you didn't,' he rasped harshly, 'you were too busy thinking of your own bloody self—like all women. Dammit, Caron, the least you could have done was left a note.'

'You went out yesterday without telling me where you were going,' she said defensively.

His eyes flashed his fury. 'So that's why you did it?'

'Of course not, but as far as I knew you were going to be out all day and I wanted some fresh air. You're being totally unfair. If you insist on leaving me to my own devices then you shouldn't complain if I go out.'

Suddenly the anger died out of his eyes, replaced with a gleam of pleasure. His lips lost their hardness and curved into a smile, his whole body relaxed. 'As always, Caron, you're very beautiful when you're angry.'

Unlike you, she thought bitterly. He was frightening when he built himself up into a rage. His whole body stiffened and he towered threateningly over her and she sometimes feared for her safety. Though to give him his due he had never actually touched her in anger. Now he was charming Dr Jekyll again. The monstrous Mr Hyde had disappeared, though who knew for how long?

'I have an urge to make love to you that can't wait,' he muttered thickly.

And that was all he really wanted her for. Caron felt tears prick the backs of her eyelids and she rapidly blinked them away. 'I need a bath; I'm tired and sticky after walking around all day.' She headed for the stairs.

'You're tired!' His loud voice arrested her and suddenly he was angry again. '*You're tired*! After being married for two days I'm getting excuses. I'm afraid that's not good enough, Caron. You're my wife and I want you—now.'

'I didn't say I wouldn't let you make love to me,' she responded without looking at him, her heart pounding at the very thought. 'I simply need to freshen myself up.'

His eyes glittered again suddenly. 'Then we'll bathe together. Have you ever done that, Caron, taken a bath with a man? Did the unfortunate Karl, in his first flush of enthusiasm, ever make such a suggestion?'

Caron felt her cheeks grow warm but she kept her voice deliberately cool. 'Indeed not.'

He laughed at her indignation and, stepping forward, swept her into his arms. Caron felt the steady beat of his heart as he carried her upstairs.

Excitement rather than intimidation built up inside her, and by the time he reached their bedroom she felt as breathless as if she had run up the stairs herself.

He put her down, gazed for a moment into the brilliant green of her eyes, and with a murmured, 'I won't be long,' crossed to the bathroom. Within seconds she heard water gushing out of the taps and caught a waft of exotic fragrance.

When he came back she was still standing where he had left her, feeling slightly bemused by the unexpected turn of events and the speed with which he was carrying out his threat. If threat was the right word? Perhaps not. To threaten meant an intention to punish or hurt. Lawson wasn't going to hurt her. It was a promise. A promise of a pleasurable experience. And suddenly there was a race going on inside her as her pulses went into high gear.

'You're very desirable, Caron,' he muttered as he stood in front of her. He touched her cheek with a gentle finger and caused a storm inside her! The clear blue of his eyes was much darker than normal and for a few seconds his gaze held hers, triggering fresh emotions, and then, as his fingers trailed down the column of her throat, his eyes followed the same path.

She was wearing a red woollen coat dress and with excruciating slowness he began to unbutton it, kissing each inch of flesh as it was exposed. Caron did not know how she managed to stand there without giving herself away. She wanted to help him, she wanted to rip her dress off quickly, his clothes too, she wanted the excitement of feeling his hair-roughened male body against hers.

But she made herself stand still and pretend indifference, though Lawson would have to be totally insensitive not to feel the unusual warmth of her skin or observe the throbbing of her pulses.

'Your turn now,' he said hoarsely.

It took her a second or two to realise that he was inviting her to undress him. She wanted to refuse and yet she didn't. She wanted to disrobe him and yet was afraid, afraid of the feelings that were flaring within her.

With uncanny accuracy Lawson read her thoughts. 'What's wrong,' he mocked, 'are you afraid? Have you never undressed a man before?' He reached out and took her hands, putting them on the buttons of his shirt, and after that Caron's own senses took over.

She stripped off his shirt and ran her hands over the hard planes of his chest and back, kissing him, rubbing her own breasts against him, touching her teeth to his nipples, hearing his sharp indrawn breath and feeling sudden tension run through him. She had never done anything like this to a man before and yet seemed to know instinctively what he would like. It was a heady sensation that she had the power to arouse him like this.

Next she undid the clip on his trousers and slid down the zip. He kicked off his shoes in readiness and as he stepped out of his grey mohair trousers Caron felt wave after wave of hunger engulf her. She wanted this man so much, so very, very much. It was a physical longing that she had never thought possible. She had never dreamt that such intense feelings existed before meeting Lawson. She hoped he wouldn't delay the moment too long.

CHAPTER NINE

CARON knew that she must have given herself away. Either that or she had given Lawson the opinion that she enjoyed sex for the sake of sex. Bathing with Lawson and making love had been an experience to surpass all experiences, better even than on their wedding night, when she had thought nothing could outdo it.

In the bath they had uninhibitedly explored each other's bodies, playing and splashing, rolling over like porpoises, laughing one minute, serious the next. He had made love to her in the water and out of it. On the bed, on the floor, standing up. They were both inexhaustible and could not get enough of each other.

It was early morning before they finally dropped into an exhausted sleep and now Caron was lying at Lawson's side, having woken as the sun tinged the sky pink, wondering what the outcome of it all would be. Would he slide out of bed if she pretended to be asleep and go to work without speaking to her again? The thought that it was only at times like this that they were close crucified her. She did not want him to need her for her body alone.

You knew it when he asked you to marry him, reminded her conscience. But it made no difference. She had thought a good physical relationship would be enough to begin with, but it wasn't. She wanted Lawson's mind as well as his body. She wanted them to be friends, to be close at all times, she wanted him to share his problems, tell her about his work, talk about all manner of things. She craved all of him—now!

Sleep claimed her again and when she awoke the sun was well risen and Lawson had left. A glance at the clock told her that it was after nine so she could not blame him for going, but he could have woken her and kissed her goodbye. Her body still glowed with the aftermath of their lovemaking and a few warm words this morning would have made all the difference.

Finding a note on the kitchen table caused her a few seconds' happiness until she read it. 'Caron, Mrs Blake has hurt her back so won't be in for a few days. L.' It couldn't have been more impersonal. There were no words at all to remind her of their erotic experiences last night.

Disappointment welled up thick and fast and she banged her fist on the table in anger. How dared he treat her like this and then expect her to fall into his arms when he wanted to make love? It was inhuman. She wouldn't co-operate any more. And yet she knew she would. He only had to look at her and she felt herself melting. She shook her head furiously. It was a crazy situation.

Caron made herself a cup of tea and sat sipping it. She would do the housework today and cook their meal, maybe even do some washing. And perhaps when Lawson came home he would be friendly and she could pretend there was nothing wrong with their marriage.

Halfway through the morning the phone rang and it was Stephanie. 'Caron, I don't know whether to tell you off or give you my congratulations.'

'You've heard?'

'Indeed I have, just a few minutes ago through a friend of a friend who happens to work for Lawson. I've phoned that no-good brother-in-law of mine and given him a piece of my mind. Wait till Bruce hears. He'll go mad that his own brother has remarried without a word to anyone. I had no idea you two felt this way about each other; you never let on when we met.'

'We hadn't discovered our feelings then,' excused Caron.

'But when you did you couldn't wait to get married? How romantic. Can I come and see you? You must be feeling awfully lonely with Lawson back at work—I told him off about that as well.'

'I'd love you to come,' confessed Caron, wondering how Lawson had reacted to his sister-in-law's chastisement. He probably hadn't minded; he was too fond of Stephanie to let anything she said hurt. 'But aren't you at work?'

'Not any more,' Stephanie disclosed. 'I'm pregnant, Caron. Only three months but I've decided to give up my job.' The excitement in her voice was unmistakable.

'Oh, Stephanie, congratulations. That's wonderful news.'

'We think so too,' she laughed. 'I'll be there as soon as I can. How's your brother, by the way?'

'Almost fully recovered, thank goodness,' Caron told her. She had rung John the other night while waiting for Lawson and he'd sounded so happy that she envied him. It seemed everyone was happy but herself.

When Stephanie arrived she took her through into the sitting-room so that they could sit and look out at the garden. This had quickly become Caron's favourite spot.

'Lawson had no right going straight back to work without taking you on honeymoon,' said Stephanie, settling herself into her seat. 'Honestly, the man has no soul.'

'Did you tell him that as well?' laughed Caron. The auburn-haired girl was so indignant.

'I told him everything, believe me. I wouldn't have been surprised to find him back here apologising to you.' Then she grimaced wryly. 'On the other hand, his work does mean a lot to him. That's why I can't understand why he stayed away for so long. In one way I'm glad he did, though, because if he hadn't he wouldn't have met you. He deserves some happiness in his life. I hope we're going to be good friends.'

'I'm sure we will,' Caron agreed. 'And I'm dying to meet Bruce as well. Why don't you come round for a meal one evening?'

'Try keeping us away,' grinned Stephanie. 'But not yet, not at the honeymoon stage. I imagine when Lawson does come home you spend most of your time in bed?'

Caron coloured delicately, giving herself away, even though she said, 'No, really, I'd like you to come.'

'In that case I'll wait eagerly for your invitation. What do you think of this house?'

'It's all right,' shrugged Caron, wondering if it would be too disloyal to criticise it.

'But there are too many reminders of Lawson's first wife?' suggested Stephanie astutely.

Caron nodded. 'I don't think either of us really likes it. It's too—oh, I don't know, I just think a little cottage somewhere would be much nicer.'

'And that's what Lawson would like as well?'

'I think so,' she answered quietly, 'even though he's told me to go ahead and redecorate. I don't actually think it would make much difference. The feeling in the house isn't right.'

'I know exactly what you mean,' said Stephanie. 'It was a pity he ever sold his father's cottage. You'd have liked that. It had loads of character.'

'I'd love to see it,' said Caron impulsively, feeling it would help her get a better insight into this man she had married.

'Then why don't we drive out right now and take a look?' suggested Stephanie, her excitement matching Caron's.

No sooner was the thought born than they were on their way. Twelve miles out of Dublin they were in the heart of the countryside, with heathlands and peat-bogs, forests of pine and larch and fir, scattered cottages and even a disused monastery. The lush beauty of the Irish countryside never ceased to impress Caron.

On the outskirts of a village in County Wicklow was an enchanting whitewashed cottage with a thatched roof and a pink front door. 'This is it,' said Stephanie, stopping the car and getting out. To the surprise of both of them it was up for sale.

'Oh, Stephanie,' said Caron, 'let's ask if we can look around.' This was something she had never expected.

The garden gate, painted pink also, hung on its hinges and the garden itself was sadly neglected, though Caron could see how beautiful it must once have been. It was the typical cottage garden Lawson had described with hollyhocks and roses and marguerites and fuchsias and dozens of other flowers in various stages of bloom.

To her intense disappointment there was no one at home; in fact it looked as though no one lived there any more, and the estate agents were ironically back in Dublin. 'I'll get the keys tomorrow and come back,' said Caron enthusiastically. 'Will you drive me?'

'Willingly,' enthused Stephanie.

Caron did not tell Lawson that she had been out but she did tell him that Stephanie had telephoned.

'Yes, she phoned me as well,' he admitted. 'That woman certainly knows how to tear a strip off a fellow.' But he was smiling as he said it. Clearly Stephanie could do no wrong in his eyes. Caron wished he had the same affection for her.

'I thought I'd ask her and Bruce over for dinner one evening.'

Lawson nodded. 'An excellent idea. How about tomorrow?'

Caron was stunned that he had agreed so readily, but delighted also.

She had roasted a chicken for their dinner, which she served with plenty of fresh vegetables and sage and onion stuffing. Lawson ate every bit, but he was deeply withdrawn and as soon as he had finished he announced that he had brought some work home and would be shutting himself in his study for the rest of the evening.

Caron had thought that after last night, when they had been so close, he might spend some time with her, time when they could talk and learn more about each other. It was almost as if Lawson was deliberately trying to avoid any such moments.

'Can I help you in any way?' she asked, and when he shook his head it confirmed her suspicions that all he wanted was her body.

'Can't I at least sit in with you? I'll be very quiet.'

'No, Caron, this work needs all my concentration.' There was a biting edge to his voice which told her clearly that she was annoying him and it would be wise to shut up.

'I feel as though I'm in solitary confinement,' she muttered beneath her breath but he heard and he frowned.

'Is that how you see it, Caron?'

'Yes, I do,' she told him frankly, her chin jutting. 'Don't you realise that I feel trapped? I can't get out unless I walk, and when you do come home you don't want my company. I'd like to know what's wrong. Why did you marry me if you're going to treat me like this?'

He closed his eyes and drew in a deep breath. When he looked at her again there was no expression at all on his face. 'I married you because I—need you, Caron.'

'To fulfil your carnal desires,' she spat, suddenly angry.

'And yours,' he retorted sharply.

'And that's really all our marriage means? You're satisfied with the fact that we're good in bed?'

'It's a beginning, or at least I thought it was.'

There was an innuendo behind his words and she frowned but he gave her no time to puzzle over it.

'I didn't realise it wasn't enough. You're not the girl I thought you were, Caron.' His jaw grew taut as he spoke, his eyes hard, and without another word he scraped back his chair and left the room.

Caron had no idea what he was talking about and she felt suddenly ice-cold, as though she had been standing in a deep-freeze for several hours. She wrapped her arms about her and sat shivering. This marriage simply wasn't going to work, she could see that now. Lawson was a much more complex man than she had thought. Never in a hundred years would she begin to understand him.

Josie had had a dishwasher installed but Mrs Blake ignored it and so did Caron; washing up by hand gave her something to do. Even so the evening stretched interminably ahead. She read a magazine for a while but went to bed early, and was fast asleep when Lawson eventually joined her.

Although she was awake when he got up she kept her eyes closed and did not move until he had left the house. The thought that she was going to look at Columbine Cottage today helped cheer her up and as soon as Stephanie arrived they fetched the key from the estate agent. On the way Caron invited her and Bruce to dinner that evening and Stephanie happily accepted. 'Bruce is dying to meet you.'

The cottage was bigger than Caron had expected but otherwise had the same cosy rooms and open fireplaces that she had imagined. It was still fully furnished and they had learned from the estate agent that the woman who owned the cottage had died and her family lived in America. They wanted it sold as it stood.

Caron could imagine Lawson living here as a boy, playing in the garden, paddling in the stream at the bottom of it, and as he grew older dedicatedly looking after his sister. Why, oh, why had he let Josie persuade him to sell? It must have been heart-rending.

In that instant she made up her mind that somehow, some way, she would get this cottage back for Lawson. This would be her way of telling him that she loved him. And if that didn't work nothing would and she might as well give up the whole idea of being Mrs Lawson Savage.

Stephanie had an appointment at the antenatal clinic so they didn't stop long and she dropped Caron off at the bottom of the drive. 'I'll see you tonight,' she confirmed cheerfully.

Caron also felt in a much happier mood and was humming softly as she let herself into the house. She was shocked to discover Lawson yet again waiting in the hall. His eyes held a dangerous, glittering hardness that sent an icy chill shivering down her spine. 'Where the hell have you been?' he rasped. 'Whose car was that I saw you getting out of? No, don't tell me, it was some man you've picked up, wasn't it? If that's what you want then you can damn well go to him. You can pack your bags right this minute and leave.'

Caron stared at Lawson for several panicky seconds. He couldn't mean it. He wasn't turning her out just because he *assumed* she had been out with another man. 'You're wrong,' she protested, 'I haven't been out with any man. I wouldn't do a thing like that.'

'No?' he sneered. 'Then suppose you tell me who it is you've been seeing these last two days? Oh, yes, I know all about yesterday as well. I telephoned home several times and there was no answer. But not a word last night, nothing except a constant stream of complaints because I put my work before you. Who the hell is he, Caron?'

Caron was tempted not to tell him. If he couldn't trust her then that was his fault. Only the fact that she loved him so much and would go to any lengths to win his love made her swallow her pride and look him straight in the eye. 'As a matter of fact I've been out with Stephanie.'

'Stephanie?' he echoed, his blue eyes disbelieving. His sister-in-law was obviously the last person in the world he had expected her to say.

'That's right,' she confirmed brittlely. 'We've had lunch together. She felt sorry for me, being left here by myself. But you wouldn't understand that, would you? The most important thing in your life is your job. A wife comes a poor second. It's a pity I didn't know that before I married you.'

'Wouldn't it have been courteous to let me know what you were doing?'

Caron glared at him angrily. 'If this were a normal marriage, then yes, I would have done, but as you've made it quite clear that you don't care a fig about me, why should I bother about you?'

A muscle clenched in his jaw. 'I wouldn't have married you if I hadn't cared about you, Caron.'

But he didn't love her! And that was what hurt most of all. 'This conversation's getting us nowhere,' she snapped coldly. 'If you'll excuse me I'd like to go and take a shower—unless you still wish me to leave?'

She paused within inches of him, her green eyes flashing into his blue ones, testing him, yet dreading the thought that he might say yes. She was close enough to feel the warmth of his body and dangerous sensations ran through her limbs.

When his arms shot around her she was totally unprepared, and when his mouth claimed hers in a kiss that was punishing yet sensual she almost gave in to the needs of her body—almost but not quite. She could not forget his condemning face as she had walked through the doorway, the accusations he was so ready to make.

With a strength of will Caron had not known she possessed she stood still in his arms, her lips inflexible beneath his, and when he flung her from him in disgust she marched upstairs with her head held high and tears coursing down her cheeks.

In seconds she had stripped off her clothes and was standing beneath the fierce jets of the shower. She stayed there for a long time, trying to defuse the anger which had built up inside her. Or was it disappointment because Lawson had judged her so harshly? Did he really think she would go out with another man? Did he think she was the same as Josie and his mother? Did he really know so little about her?

When she came out Lawson was sitting on the edge of the bed. Her heartbeats accelerated as she pulled the towel more closely around her. She felt vulnerable, far too vulnerable.

'Whose idea was it that you go out with Stephanie, hers or yours?'

'So we're back to that, are we?' she asked crisply. 'Does it really matter whose idea it was?'

There were splinters of ice in his eyes. 'It might interest you to know that I don't care to have details of my private life spread out to all and sundry.'

'Your family are not all and sundry,' she pointed out, stepping back a pace as he rose from the bed, feeling excitement run through her veins despite the fact that he was looking at her as though she were beyond contempt.

'Families are worse. Families interfere. Stephanie's already told me off.'

'Yes, I know,' she told him impatiently, 'and can you blame her? But actually I haven't said a thing, even though our marriage is anything but normal and I don't know why I ever agreed to it.'

'You must have had a reason?' His eyes narrowed as he waited for her answer.

And if she told him why, if she told him that she loved him but his attitude was driving her crazy, what would he say then? Would he laugh in her face and tell her she was a fool, that she had known all along that he would never love her? She swallowed hard. 'I thought we might have been friends as well as enjoying a good physical relationship, but it hasn't turned out that way. You spend all your time working and leave me to my own devices. You won't even accept any offers of help.'

'I have my reasons,' he told her, 'and what I want now is your assurance that you won't go running around the countryside without letting me know where you are.'

'You mean you want to keep tabs on me?' she asked crossly.

'I mean I worry about you. You have no friends in this area, it's very difficult for you, I appreciate that. Why don't you get on with doing up the house?'

'Because I don't like this damned house,' she flashed back.

He stilled a moment and looked at her closely. 'If that's true then we'll sell and move somewhere else. To that cottage you so romantically dream about.'

Caron smiled. 'Do you mean that?'

'Yes, if it's going to make you happy. Phone a few estate agents, see what's for sale. I'll leave everything up to you.'

He had said more or less the same thing to Josie, she thought, and look what had happened. But he wouldn't be sorry this time. Little did he know that he had just made her dream come true, he had made everything easy for her. She wanted to run to him and kiss him and feel his arms around her, but already, tired of the conversation, he was leaving the room. She swallowed her disappointment. 'You haven't forgotten that your brother and Stephanie are coming to dinner tonight?'

It was clear by his expression that it had slipped his mind. He turned sharply, a frown creasing his brow. 'I'll be in my study. Let me know when they arrive.'

Caron enjoyed cooking. She had always helped her mother at home and even in the flat she had been nominated chief cook as neither of the girls she shared with were any good at it. Occasionally they had entertained and then she had really gone to town. Now she was glad that Mrs Blake wasn't here because it meant that she could do everything herself.

The meal was all planned in her mind: thin melon slices to start with, arranged in a fan shape with raspberry sauce, medallions of beef for their main course with another sauce—this time Roquefort cheese—and to follow either fresh fruit salad or cheese and biscuits— or both!

It was a menu she was familiar with so she didn't need to spend her time poring over a cook-book, and she had everything prepared in plenty of time to get herself ready.

Although Lawson had instructed her to fetch him from his study she heard him go upstairs long before his brother was due and he appeared in the kitchen freshly showered and dressed in grey mohair trousers and a pale blue silk shirt. His Paisley patterned tie was in delicate shades of lavender, grey and blue. Very discreet but very tasteful. A musky aftershave she hadn't known him use before wafted beneath her nostrils, and the very sight of him set every nerve-end quivering in response.

'Something smells good,' he acknowledged, but there was no smile on his face. He was obviously still angry with her.

'It's nice to have an opportunity to cook. I enjoy it.'

'Are you suggesting I get rid of Mrs Blake?'

Caron saw the sudden flare of his nostrils and shook her head. 'Of course not.'

'That's good, because the job is hers for as long as she wants it,' he said crisply.

To Caron's relief the doorbell rang, announcing the arrival of their guests. She took in a long, much needed breath of air and went forward with him to greet them.

Bruce was nothing like Lawson. Caron had imagined a man of similar build with the same curly black hair. Although he was tall he was reed-thin, and his hair was a mousy brown and already receding, even though he was younger than Lawson. He had the same strong jawline, however, and blue eyes which were laughing and friendly.

The two men held each other in an embrace that spoke a thousand words. It was the first time they had met since Lawson had gone away after Emily died, and now Josie was dead too and there was so much that needed to be said but was too painful.

Then Bruce turned to Caron and hugged her too. 'So we meet at last. Stephanie's told me so much about you. I couldn't believe Lawson had got married again, but now I can see why.' He turned again to his brother. 'You're a lucky fellow.'

'Indeed I am,' said Lawson, and much to Caron's surprise his arm came about her shoulders and he smiled at her fondly. 'My life changed when I met this young lady.'

And for the rest of the evening he was more attentive than he had ever been, touching her hand, kissing her, looking at her constantly. Although Caron knew it was all an act, put on for Bruce and Stephanie's benefit, she could not help responding. Her face glowed, her eyes shone, and her whole body was filled with sensation. How wonderful life would be, she thought, if he was always like this.

When Stephanie helped carry the plates out to the kitchen she said, 'I've never seen Lawson look so happy.

You really are perfect for each other. I'm so pleased for both of you.'

Caron smiled. 'I love him so much.' It was the first time she had said the words out loud and she felt faintly shy for admitting it.

But Stephanie nodded. 'You don't have to tell me—I know. It's written all over your face, Lawson's too.'

What would the other girl say, thought Caron, if she knew it was all an act? That in actual fact Lawson felt no love for her at all? She could only hope that once they were in the cottage everything would be all right. It was a dream she intended clinging to, come what may. Tonight was a bonus but it wouldn't last.

It lasted long enough, though, for their lovemaking that night to be more intense and more magical than ever. If she hadn't known differently Caron would have said Lawson did actually love her. He seemed to be worshipping her body, and his eyes when he looked into hers were full of love also, or was it just desire again and she was imagining it?

Nevertheless she felt as if she were floating on cloud nine and she did not want to come back down to earth. If only the other side of their life could be this good, she thought, lying in his arms afterwards, listening to his deepened breathing. She did not know how he could enjoy moments like this and then practically ignore her at other times.

She hoped and prayed that tomorrow would be different, that this was the beginning of a new phase in their life, but when she awoke nothing had changed. The bed was cold and empty at her side, telling her that Lawson had left many hours ago. She felt hurt, deeply hurt, because it meant that once again he had used her. But then she thought of the cottage and what it would be like if she was able to buy it, and suddenly she felt happy again.

On the kitchen table was a note, weighted down with a set of keys. Frowning slightly, Caron picked up the sheet of paper. 'In the garage is something that will help you in your search for the ideal cottage. L.'

Did he mean what she thought? Caron rushed through the house to the internal door that led into the large three-car garage and there, standing all by itself, was a brand new sparkling Alfa Romeo. She stood transfixed for several seconds. Lawson had come home early yesterday especially to give it to her and she had been out. No wonder he had been so upset.

But later, when Stephanie and Bruce had been and gone, why hadn't he told her then? Caron decided she would never understand the way his mind worked. But it did show a whole new side of Lawson and she began to wonder whether she wasn't misjudging him.

She visited the estate agent and told him that she wanted to buy Columbine Cottage and put their own house on the market. It was a very bold move, she knew, but Lawson had told her to go ahead so she ignored her misgivings.

'We actually have a client who's looking for a house like the one you want to sell,' the man told her. 'If he likes it then the sale could go through very quickly. Are you any relation to the Savages who used to live in Columbine Cottage?'

'I'm married to Lawson Savage, who was the previous owner,' she told him. 'We want to move back into it. Well, at least I know Lawson would like to but I haven't told him it's up for sale. I want it to be a surprise. Will that be any problem?'

'Not if he's given you the authority to buy it in your name, otherwise it will need his signature.'

'He says I can do what I like,' Caron admitted happily. She didn't think he'd mind; they could always change it into his name or joint names afterwards. 'How long will it take, do you think? I want to get it decorated and furnished ready to move in once the other house is sold.'

Mr Brown smiled at her enthusiasm. 'I think you could be in luck, my dear. A previous purchaser dropped out at the last minute. Ross, the solicitor next door, had already done most of the paperwork. If you use him it shouldn't take much more than a week—provided you have the money, of course; otherwise I'm afraid you'll have to wait until your other house is sold.'

Caron hadn't thought of the money aspect but she wasn't unduly alarmed. 'There'll be no problem,' she told him airily, and kept her fingers mentally crossed that Lawson would agree to pay, that he could actually afford it.

She could not wait for him to come home and was acutely disappointed when he turned up with his accountant. 'I've brought Fielding home to go over some figures,' he told her. 'Can you stretch the dinner to three?'

Guy Fielding did not leave until well after midnight and although Caron had gone to bed she was still wide awake and sitting up waiting for Lawson. She wore a delicate pink nightdress which revealed rather than concealed.

'I want to thank you for the car,' she said. 'It's a beauty, I really love it.'

'If it makes you happy then that's all that matters,' he answered gruffly as though her enthusiasm embarrassed him. 'You didn't have to lie awake just to tell me that, but I'm glad you did.' He took off his shirt with indecent haste and was unzipping his trousers when Caron spoke again.

'There's something else I want to talk about,' she said hesitantly.

'Won't it wait? God, Caron, you shouldn't sit there looking so desirable. Haven't you any idea what you do to me?'

'No, I mean yes, but I want to talk now, Lawson, it's important. I've—I've seen a cottage I like and, well, there's a chance I could get the keys within a week if—if we have the money to pay for it.'

He frowned in sudden astonishment. 'What the hell's the rush?'

'It—it needs things doing to it. I thought it would keep me busy sorting everything out, and then we could—move in as soon as this house is sold.' Caron's only fear was that he might say he wanted to see the cottage first.

'It's what you want?' he asked.

Caron nodded.

'Don't you think you ought to look around some more?'

'I've fallen in love with it.'

'You'll be happy there, even when I'm at work?'

She nodded again.

'Very well, but you do realise I haven't time to look at it myself? I'll have to trust your judgement.'

'I think you'll like it too,' she whispered shyly.

He gave a faint nod. 'We do appear to have similar tastes in that direction. I'll give you a cheque, and open you an account for anything else that you might need—furniture, that sort of stuff. Don't take anything from here, for God's sake—except my Monet,' he added with a wry smile.

Caron was over the moon with happiness but did not dare show it too much. She did not want him getting suspicious. He had to still think that she hated this house and anywhere would be better. When he made love to her afterwards she responded with even more fervour than usual.

The next morning she telephoned Stephanie and told her the good news. 'I can't believe it,' the girl laughed. 'You're more devious than I thought. But it's wonderful. And you're sure Lawson has no idea?'

'None at all; he's simply not interested. But I need your help, Stephanie. I want to decorate and furnish it as closely as possible to when Lawson lived there. Can you remember what it was like?'

'Can I remember?' scoffed Stephanie. 'My dear girl, I have a photographic memory. A week you say, before you get the keys? That's unheard of. We'll spend the time looking for the right bits and pieces of furniture. We're going to have a ball.'

'So long as you don't overdo it in your condition,' warned Caron.

'I'm as fit as a fiddle,' her sister-in-law assured her, and when they met later Caron had never seen her so radiant. One day perhaps she would be that happy too. It was a thought she clung to as if it were a lifeline.

During the next few weeks Caron's time was fully taken up with the cottage. She refused to get in a firm of decorators, telling herself it would be too expensive, and did all the painting and paper-hanging herself, although she always made sure that she was home and had Lawson's dinner cooked by the time he came in. He never worked late these days, although he always brought work home and spent the evenings in his study.

'How's the cottage coming on?' he asked her one night, much to her surprise. It was the first interest he had shown.

To her chagrin she felt guilty colour suffuse her cheeks. 'I'm getting there slowly,' she said.

'What do you mean, *you're* getting there? You're surely not working on it yourself?'

'Well, yes, I am,' she confessed.

'God, girl, if you're that short of money, you should ask. I'm hardly a pauper.' His blue eyes blazed into hers.

'It only needs decorating,' she protested quickly, 'and I'm enjoying it, really I am. It's something I've found a flair for.'

His frown still persisted. 'Perhaps I should come and take a look at this cottage?'

And ruin her surprise, thought Caron in horror.

'I don't want you wearing yourself out,' he added.

'Wearing myself out?' Caron felt suddenly angry that he should show concern at this stage when he was the one who never cared about what she did, when he was the one who left her to twiddle her thumbs all day long. But she was careful to keep the anger out of her voice. 'It's fun. I'm truly enjoying it.'

'I still think I ought to——'

'Lawson, please,' cut in Caron, 'I'm not doing too much, and I'm confident you'll be pleased with the result. Please wait until it's finished.' She gave a shy smile. 'I'd like it to be a surprise.'

'If you're sure,' he said doubtfully.

'I am.'

He looked at her for a long, silent moment. 'It means a lot to you, this cottage, doesn't it?'

She nodded.

'Come here, Caron.'

With her heart singing she walked into his arms. He held her close and for once his embrace did not culminate in making love. For the first time there was a feeling of unity, of real affection. Caron felt that at long last she was actually beginning to mean something to him.

Although the embrace was disappointingly brief it was the beginning of a turning-point in their relationship, she felt sure, and when he disappeared into his study she did not feel quite so unloved.

Caron pushed herself hard to get the cottage ready before the sale on their house was completed. Stephanie occasionally accompanied her but Caron would not let her do any climbing or strenuous work.

'You're as bad as Bruce,' complained Stephanie with a smile. 'He pampers me to death. Anyone would think I was the first woman ever to have a baby.'

'If anything happened to you I would never forgive myself,' said Caron from her perch on a pair of steps. This was the last of the three bedrooms and she was painting the ceiling in palest lemon. But as she looked down at Stephanie she felt strangely dizzy. The room began to whirl and her legs buckled beneath her.

'Caron!' shrieked Stephanie in horror, but there was nothing she could do to save her, Caron was already hitting the floor.

CHAPTER TEN

FORTUNATELY Caron was not badly hurt by the fall. She was bruised and shaken, but no bones were broken. 'What happened?' asked Stephanie, looking shaken herself by the accident.

Caron shook her head. 'I don't know, I felt dizzy, that's all.'

'You've been overdoing it,' admonished the auburn-haired girl severely. 'Sit down while I make you some tea.'

'I really feel all right again now,' protested Caron, but Stephanie insisted.

For the rest of the day Caron worked at a more leisurely pace. Stephanie wanted her to go home and rest but she refused, saying that she was fussing for nothing. But when she did get home she ached miserably and instead of her usual quick shower she ran a bath and lay soaking in the scented water.

'Caron, wake up. Caron!'

She had not heard Lawson come in and she looked at him now with startled eyes. 'You're early,' she accused.

'No, I'm not,' he rasped harshly, angrily, 'you've fallen asleep. My God, Caron, what an insane thing to do.'

Caron shivered. She must have been here for a long time because the water was cold. She had thought to shut her eyes only for a few seconds.

'Are you ill? You look as though you haven't the strength to even stand,' he growled, and held out his hand.

Too cold to sit and argue, Caron allowed him to help her out, but she was unprepared for his bellow of anger. 'What the hell have you done to your back?'

Caron guessed she must have bruised it when she fell, and cursed her insanity at letting him catch her like this. 'I bumped it against the step-ladder,' she said. 'It's nothing.'

'Nothing?' he roared. 'Have you seen it? That wasn't caused by a mere bump. Caron, what happened?'

'I'm cold,' she said, 'can't the interrogation wait?'

Immediately he cocooned her in a large, fluffy grey towel and began rubbing her dry, taking care not to touch the tender part of her back. Caron still felt achy and her head swam and for once she felt no response to his nearness. 'I think I'd like to go to bed,' she whispered, and then fainted in his arms.

Caron was aware of the soft words of a doctor, of riding in an ambulance, of hospital corridors and nurses, and bed, and sleep, and seeing Lawson white-faced and worried. Finally her mind cleared and she looked about the clinical room and wondered what she was doing here. It was clearly a private ward and Lawson sat beside her looking grim and tired, but when he saw she was awake he allowed himself a faint smile. 'How are you feeling?'

'All right, I think,' she said. 'What happened?'

'You fainted.'

'But why am I here?' And why was he looking so angry? He was doing his hardest to hide it but she could see it there in his eyes, eyes that were red-rimmed and sore through lack of sleep.

'You really don't know?'

Caron shook her head. 'I fell off some steps, I remember, but everything else is a blur.'

'You damn well did fall,' he told her harshly, 'I got the whole sorry story out of Stephanie—how you've been pushing yourself so hard, just for the sake of some damn cottage. Well, to hell with the cottage, Caron, you can forget it, do you hear that? Forget it!'

Caron flinched back against her pillows and at that moment a nurse, having heard Lawson's raised voice, came hurrying into the room. She took one look at Lawson and asked him to leave. 'We can't have you upsetting your wife at a time like this.'

After that one of the doctors came to see her. 'You really are a very lucky young woman. You could have quite easily lost your baby. No more decorating, do you hear? You're to take it easy for the next few weeks.'

Caron looked at him blankly. 'Baby? I'm pregnant! Is that what you're saying?'

'You didn't know?' An eyebrow rose in surprise.

'I had no idea.' For a week or two now she'd had a vague feeling of not being well, but she had put it down to the work she was doing on the cottage and the fact that she was unhappy with her relationship with Lawson. How could she have been so naïve? Did she really think they could have made love as many times as they had without her getting pregnant? 'Have you told my husband?'

The doctor nodded. 'Naturally.'

Caron did not ask how he had taken it. She had seen for herself how angry he was. Tears welled up and rolled down her cheeks before she could contain them. 'I'm sorry if I'm being childish,' she said, 'but I can't help it.'

'It's understandable to be emotional at a time like this.' His smile was deeply comforting. 'And you'll be fine so long as you do as you're told and get plenty of rest.'

When he had gone the nurse came back in. 'I think you should try to get some sleep,' she said firmly. 'I'll tell your husband to go home and come back later.'

Caron nodded. She did not want to face Lawson again, not yet, not until she felt strong enough to stand up to him. Not until she had grown used to the idea of what had happened.

The next time she awoke Stephanie was sitting by her bed, a very worried Stephanie. 'Oh, Caron,' she said, taking her hand. 'Are you all right?'

Caron swallowed hard and nodded but could not stem her tears. She had been dreaming about the baby; she had seen it floating away from her and Lawson had been running to catch it but always it was just out of his reach. She hoped it did not mean that she was going to lose the baby.

'If only I'd known, I'd have never let you do all that work.'

'If I'd known I wouldn't have done it either,' she grimaced. 'Lawson—Lawson's very angry with me.' Her voice broke as she spoke and more tears coursed down her cheeks, falling in damp spots on the pristine white pillow. 'He doesn't want children. He——'

'Doesn't want children?' interrupted Stephanie, her beautiful eyes wide. 'Lawson adores children. Whatever gave you that idea?'

'Something he once said.'

'Probably when he was in one of his black moods,' commented Stephanie wryly. 'He wouldn't mean it.'

Caron wasn't so sure. 'He's even talking about getting rid of the cottage.'

'Oh, no!' exclaimed Stephanie. 'Not after all your hard work. Have you told him it's Columbine?'

'No, have you?'

Stephanie shook her head.

'I'm not going to give it up, no matter what he says,' said Caron grimly. 'I'll stall for time, get someone to finish the work and hope he'll change his mind when he sees it.'

'I'm sure he will,' said Stephanie. 'There's no way he'll be able to resist it.'

Caron wished she had her sister-in-law's confidence.

Lawson did not come back until early evening. Caron heard his footsteps in the corridor outside and waited with bated breath to see what sort of mood he was in. To her relief the aggressiveness seemed to have left him. His smile was cautious, although his hands gripped hers so hard that they hurt.

'How are you feeling, Caron?'

She smiled weakly, guiltily. 'I'm all right. Have they told you when I can go home?'

'In the morning, once the doctor's been to see you. But you must have complete rest.'

She nodded in agreement. 'I feel too tired to argue about that.'

He was silent a moment, looking down at their two hands entwined, then he said softly, 'Caron, why didn't you tell me about the baby?'

'Because I didn't know,' she replied, equally quietly. 'Do you really think I'd have worked the way I did if I had known? I wouldn't let Stephanie do anything because of her condition. I would definitely have looked after myself.'

'I thought maybe it was deliberate?' There was a narrowed intensity to his eyes. 'I thought maybe you didn't want the child because...'

When he stopped she said, 'Because of what, Lawson?' She wished she knew what he was thinking, what was going on behind those carefully controlled blue eyes.

'Because of—the type of marriage we have.'

She looked at him sharply. 'Whatever our relationship, I would never intentionally do something like that, Lawson; you can rest assured on that point.' It would have been an appropriate time to tell him that she loved him and that she was going to love the baby just as much, but there was something in his face that stopped her. He didn't want the child, despite what Stephanie had said. He did not want bonds of that sort in their marriage.

She wondered, after he had gone, whether he was still tormented by thoughts of his mother's treatment of Emily. Perhaps he did not think it fair to bring children into the world who were not planned. But if he thought she wouldn't love her own baby he was mistaken.

The next morning, when Lawson arrived to take her home, he was as considerate and attentive as any prospective father could be. But Caron knew it was all an act for the benefit of the hospital staff. There was still a barrier between them, he still kept his thoughts and feelings to himself.

The journey home was silent and as he helped her from his car Caron felt close to tears. She was carrying his baby, a part of him, and yet he persisted in distancing himself from her. If he hadn't wanted this child then he should never have made love to her in the first place; it was as simple as that.

Mrs Blake on the other hand was highly delighted and fussed and cosseted and would not let Caron raise so much as a finger. 'A baby's just what this house needs,' she kept saying.

After lunch Lawson announced, much to Caron's dismay, that he was going to the office. 'Mrs Blake will look after you,' he said, seeming not to notice her hurt face.

He could have sat with her, talked to her, at least pretended to be happy, thought Caron. He was making it as clear as the nose on his face that he did not want this baby, and if he was going to be like this for the whole of her pregnancy then she did not know how she was going to get through it.

When he came home he went through the motions of asking her how she felt but she knew he was not genuinely concerned, and when they went to bed he left her strictly alone. Caron had not expected him to make love to her, not tonight, not for a few days until she had recovered from her fall, but he could at least have put his arms around her and given her the reassurance that she needed. 'Are you blaming me for this baby?' she asked sharply. 'Don't you want it?'

'Of course I want it,' he answered, but he still lay with his back towards her.

'It's too soon, is that what you're thinking? You wanted to see whether our marriage would work?' Caron did not want to argue with him but it had to be sorted out before the rift between them became insurmountable. 'I'm sorry if that's the case, but there's nothing we can do about it, so I don't see why you're taking it out on me.'

'Hell, Caron,' he grated, 'that's not the case at all.'

'Then what's wrong? Why are you treating me like this?'

'Like what? I wasn't aware that my attitude had changed. All that's different is that I'm not making love to you, and that would hardly be right in the circumstances, don't you agree?'

'Making love doesn't harm a baby,' she told him angrily.

'I realise it's the only part of our marriage that you like,' he tossed back. 'And in a day or two, when you're rested, we'll resume our carnal pleasures.' There was a sneer in his voice as he spoke.

Caron closed her eyes and tried unsuccessfully to stem the hot tears that stung the backs of her eyelids. How could he think that of her? He was right, he hadn't changed. He was still the same cold-hearted bastard he'd been before. She ought to have taken precautions, she ought not to have let this happen. Instead of the baby bringing them together it was throwing them further apart.

Caron slept in until eleven the following morning and Lawson had long since left for the office. She felt sick with disappointment about his treatment of her. Stephanie had definitely been wrong in saying that he loved children. He had made it very evident that he did not want this one.

Mrs Blake brought her breakfast up on a tray—hot buttered toast and scrambled egg, plus a cup of camomile tea. 'Much better for you than ordinary tea, my dear.'

After she had finished Caron armed herself with the *Yellow Pages* and the telephone and had soon arranged for a firm of decorators to finish the paper-hanging at Columbine Cottage. The garden was already being set to rights by one of the neighbours who remembered the family clearly and was delighted that Lawson was moving back in.

As soon as it was completed the furniture, which she and Stephanie had spent so much time in choosing, would be put in place, and then—she would take Lawson to see it. Caron's heart missed a beat every time she thought about it, and she hoped against hope that he wouldn't again mention getting rid of the cottage before it reached this final stage.

The next few days were a nightmare. Lawson was solicitous, never failing to make sure that she had everything she wanted, but it was a duty rather than a loving act—and he still left her strictly alone in bed at night! This was what hurt most of all. She craved his arms around her, she wanted comfort and closeness, she wanted to share the pleasure of the baby with him.

Everything now hinged on the cottage. Caron had not realised quite how much she was depending on it until the day it was ready for Lawson to see. She got up extra early so that she could catch him before he went to work. 'About the cottage,' she began.

His face darkened, became as black as a thundercloud, even though this was the first time it had been mentioned since she'd come out of hospital. 'I don't want to hear about it. I want it sold, Caron. Didn't I make myself clear? We're not moving in there, not a place that almost cost me——' He stopped abruptly and got up from the table. 'Ring the estate agents today and tell them to put it back on the market.'

'No, Lawson.' Caron rose too and stood facing him. 'It still means a lot to me, and I think it's wrong of you to act so high-handedly without even seeing it.'

'You think I'll change my mind if I go there?' he sneered.

Caron swallowed hard and nodded. 'I think you might.'

'I think you don't know me very well,' he snapped, 'but, if it will satisfy you, then I'll go and have a look. What's the address?'

'I want us to go together,' she said quietly.

His blue eyes narrowed sharply on hers, then he lifted his shoulders. 'Very well, shall we go now and get it over with?'

Caron heaved a sigh of relief, but her heart was thumping painfully as they left the house. The final hurdle was yet to come.

She watched his face as she directed him and a faint frown, which had appeared when they left Dublin behind, deepened dramatically as they neared the village which had been his boyhood home. And when she told him to stop outside Columbine Cottage he shook his head in disbelief.

He got out of the car and walked along the path with the air of a man in a daze. He looked at the cheerful gardens, at the fresh paintwork and gleaming window-panes; and when she handed him the key he unlocked the front door and went inside and stood and looked—and looked—and looked.

'I can't believe it,' he said, speaking to himself, not to her, wandering from room to room, every one furnished more or less as it had been in the days when he had lived there, going upstairs and looking in each of the bedrooms.

Caron let him walk around on his own, sensing his deep emotion, keeping her fingers mentally crossed that this would be the turning-point in their lives.

When he came back to her tears were running unashamedly down his cheeks. He put his hands on her shoulders. 'You did this for me, Caron?'

Painfully she nodded.

'You went to all this trouble just for me?' he asked in wonder. 'Why?'

'I did it,' she said slowly, 'because—because I——' It was now or never. 'I thought it would be the best way of showing how much I—I love you.'

For several seconds he looked at her uncomprehendingly, and then, in a voice completely choked with emotion, he said, 'You—love me? You love me, Caron? God, I don't believe it. I can't believe it.' He turned away. 'It can't be true.'

Caron touched him and felt his whole body shaking. 'Please, Lawson, it is true. And all I wanted was to earn your love too; that's all I've ever wanted.'

'Earn it?' He swung around then, his eyes glazed with disbelief, and fear, and joy, and a whole host of other unreadable emotions. 'Earn it, Caron? My God, you don't have to do that—I already love you.'

She gasped and forgot to breathe, her eyes wide on his face. Her mouth fell open and she shook her head. He had treated her so badly, how could he love her?

'I love you with every fibre of my being.' His hands touched her shoulders gently, hesitantly. 'You're everything I've always looked for and never found.'

Still Caron was not sure whether to believe him. 'How can that be when——?'

'When I've treated you so contemptibly?'

She nodded.

'It was all a cover-up because I was afraid.'

'Of what?' she whispered.

'Myself. I was afraid to trust my judgement. Afraid that if I admitted my love it would crumble before my eyes. I didn't know how you felt, I had no idea that you loved me too. I thought—God, Caron, I thought all you were interested in was my body.'

'I told you from the beginning that that wasn't the case,' she reproved, though her tone was gentle.

He nodded humbly. 'I was a sick fool for not believing you. But my experience of women told me that they weren't always what they appeared. And, hell, Caron, in the beginning that's all I wanted of you, I have to be honest. I was determined to make you my lover. I had no qualms about it—until I realised that what I felt for you had grown into something more than lust.'

Caron's heart swelled with love and happiness and she put her arms around him and lifted her face to his, and the kiss he gave her was as fierce as any of the others, but this time it was given in true love. It was a long, long time before there was any movement in the cottage.

'Oh, Caron, how are you ever going to forgive me for the way I've treated you? I married you because I didn't want to let you walk out of my life and yet the instant the ceremony was over I was sure I'd done the wrong thing. I'd pressurised you into it, knowing that physically at least you couldn't resist me, but I feared I'd asked too much. I was being totally selfish, not thinking of you at all. God, I hated myself. Did you know that you loved me when you married me?'

She nodded. 'I wouldn't have agreed to it otherwise.'

'And you didn't try to get rid of the baby?'

'Oh, Lawson, no.' The truth was in Caron's eyes as she looked at him. 'I promise you I never knew I was pregnant. I thought that my body wasn't functioning properly because of all the changes in my life. As soon as I knew, I wanted the baby desperately.' She paused then went on quietly, 'I wish you felt the same. But I'm sure that——'

'Caron,' he broke in urgently, 'are you saying that you think I don't want this baby?'

She nodded unhappily.

'My dear, sweet, beautiful Caron, nothing's further from the truth, I assure you.'

'But you—you went back to work on the same day that you fetched me out of hospital. You didn't seem to care, Lawson. And ever since you've been so distant, so...'

He held her to him, his arms strong and comforting, and she felt the erratic thud of his heart. 'I couldn't show my true feelings because I didn't know how you felt. I hated the thought that I'd given you a baby you didn't want. I didn't realise, I——'

Caron silenced him with a kiss, their mouths clinging, tongues entwining, and when they finally drew apart she said softly, 'There have been so many times when I've wanted to just sit and talk and be together, to feel loved and wanted for my sake alone, not just sexually.'

'Making love with you was the only time I could let myself go,' he confessed, kissing her again, a long, mutually satisfying kiss that stopped only when they needed to draw breath. 'We have a lot of time to make up,' he said with a rueful smile. 'I love you in so many different ways. Oh, my darling, beautiful Caron, how difficult I've made life for you.'

'Shh!' She put a finger to his lips. 'No more of that. The past is over, we must live for the present. Let's be happy here in your cottage.'

'The home I never thought to see again,' he marvelled. 'How did you manage it? It's so—so perfect; everything is just as it was.'

'Stephanie helped in that direction,' she confessed. 'And talking about Stephanie, why did you let me think she was your wife?'

He grimaced. 'Some insane idea to make you jealous.'

'You certainly did that,' she admitted. 'It was on the day she turned up that I found out I loved you. My hopes were pinned on this cottage bringing us together.'

'How astute you are, my darling wife.'

'If it hadn't worked I think I'd have died. And I hope, husband of mine, that once we've moved in you won't spend so much time working?'

He grimaced painfully. 'Try keeping me away. I was a blind fool not to see that you loved me. All this time I've kept my feelings to myself, and, God, it's been hard. But not any longer. Now I want to shout my love from the roof-tops. I shall spend all of my spare time with you, with my child, my children, our children. We'll have lots of children, Caron. We'll make this cottage the happy place it should always have been.'

'And can Mrs Blake come too, to help me bring up this brood?'

'Caron.' He touched her face with a gentle but trembling finger. 'Has anyone ever told you what a remarkable woman you are?'

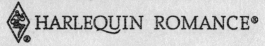

HARLEQUIN ROMANCE®

Starting in March, we are bringing you a brand-new
series—Sealed with a Kiss. We've all written SWAK at
some time on a love letter, and in these books the love
story always concerns a letter—one way or another!

We've chosen RITA nominee Leigh Michaels's
Invitation to Love (Harlequin Romance #3352)
as the first title and will be bringing you one
every month, right through to Christmas!

Watch for *Invitation to Love* by Leigh Michaels in March.
And don't miss any of these exciting Sealed with a Kiss
titles, by your favorite Harlequin Romance authors:

April	#3355	Dearest Love	Betty Neels
May	#3360	P.S. I Love You	Valerie Parv
June	#3366	Mail-Order Bridegroom	Day Leclaire
July	#3370	Wanted: Wife and Mother	Barbara McMahon

Available wherever Harlequin books are sold.

SWAK-G

HARLEQUIN ROMANCE®

brings you

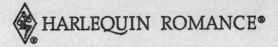

More Romances Celebrating Love, Families and Children!

Following on from Rosemary Gibson's *No Ties*, Harlequin Romance #3344, this month we're bringing you *A Valentine for Daisy*, Harlequin Romance #3347, which we know you will enjoy reading! It's a wonderful Betty Neels story, all about two adorable twins Josh and Katie who play their part in Daisy finding true love at last!

Watch out for these titles:

HARLEQUIN®

Don't miss these Harlequin favorites by some of our most distinguished authors!
And now, you can receive a discount by ordering two or more titles!

HT#25577	WILD LIKE THE WIND by Janice Kaiser	$2.99	☐
HT#25589	THE RETURN OF CAINE O'HALLORAN by JoAnn Ross	$2.99	☐
HP#11626	THE SEDUCTION STAKES by Lindsay Armstrong	$2.99	☐
HP#11647	GIVE A MAN A BAD NAME by Roberta Leigh	$2.99	☐
HR#03293	THE MAN WHO CAME FOR CHRISTMAS by Bethany Campbell	$2.89	☐
HR#03308	RELATIVE VALUES by Jessica Steele	$2.89	☐
SR#70589	CANDY KISSES by Muriel Jensen	$3.50	☐
SR#70598	WEDDING INVITATION by Marisa Carroll	$3.50 U.S. $3.99 CAN.	☐
HI#22230	CACHE POOR by Margaret St. George	$2.99	☐
HAR#16515	NO ROOM AT THE INN by Linda Randall Wisdom	$3.50	☐
HAR#16520	THE ADVENTURESS by M.J. Rodgers	$3.50	☐
HS#28795	PIECES OF SKY by Marianne Willman	$3.99	☐
HS#28824	A WARRIOR'S WAY by Margaret Moore	$3.99 U.S. $4.50 CAN.	☐

(limited quantities available on certain titles)

	AMOUNT	$
DEDUCT:	**10% DISCOUNT FOR 2+ BOOKS**	$
ADD:	**POSTAGE & HANDLING**	$
	($1.00 for one book, 50¢ for each additional)	
	APPLICABLE TAXES*	$_____
	TOTAL PAYABLE	$_____
	(check or money order—please do not send cash)	

To order, complete this form and send it, along with a check or money order for the total above, payable to Harlequin Books, to: **In the U.S.:** 3010 Walden Avenue, P.O. Box 9047, Buffalo, NY 14269-9047; **In Canada:** P.O. Box 613, Fort Erie, Ontario, L2A 5X3.

Name: _____

Address: _____ City: _____

State/Prov.: _____ Zip/Postal Code: _____

*New York residents remit applicable sales taxes.
Canadian residents remit applicable GST and provincial taxes.

HBACK-JM2

Fifty red-blooded, white-hot, true-blue hunks
from every State in the Union!

Look for MEN MADE IN AMERICA! Written by some
of our most popular authors, these stories feature some
of the strongest, sexiest men, each from a different state
in the union!

Two titles available every month at your favorite
retail outlet.

In January, look for:

WITHIN REACH by Marilyn Pappano (New Mexico)
IN GOOD FAITH by Judith McWilliams (New York)

In February, look for:

THE SECURITY MAN by Dixie Browning
(North Carolina)
A CLASS ACT by Kathleen Eagle
(North Dakota)

You won't be able to resist MEN MADE IN AMERICA!

Where do you find hot Texas nights, smooth Texas charm and dangerously sexy cowboys?

Crystal Creek reverberates with the exciting rhythm of Texas. Each story features the rugged individuals who live and love in the Lone Star state.

"...Crystal Creek wonderfully evokes the hot days and steamy nights of a small Texas community...impossible to put down until the last page is turned."
—*Romantic Times*

Praise for Bethany Campbell's *Rhinestone Cowboy*

"...this is a poignant, heart-warming story of love and redemption. One that Crystal Creek followers will wish to grab and hold on to."
—*Affaire de Coeur*

"Bethany Campbell is surely one of the brightest stars of this series."
—*Affaire de Coeur*

Don't miss the final book in this exciting series. Look for
LONESTAR STATE OF MIND by BETHANY CAMPBELL

Available in February wherever Harlequin books are sold.

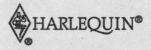